TRANSMUTATION

TRANSMUTATION

Stories

ALEX DiFRANCESCO

Seven Stories Press
New York • Oakland • London

Published by Seven Stories Press.

Library of Congress Cataloging-in-Publication Data

Names: DiFrancesco, Alex, author.
Title: Transmutation / Alex DiFrancesco.
Description: New York, NY : Seven Stories Press, [2020]
Identifiers: LCCN 2020051459 (print) | LCCN 2020051460 (ebook) | ISBN
    9781644210666 (trade paperback) | ISBN 9781644210673 (epub)
Classification: LCC PS3604.I3845 T73 2020 (print) | LCC PS3604.I3845
    (ebook) | DDC 813/.6--dc23
LC record available at https://lccn.loc.gov/2020051459
LC ebook record available at https://lccn.loc.gov/2020051460

"The Wind, the Wind" first appeared in *Signal Mountain Review*
"Perseus Denied" first appeared in *Barnhouse Journal*
"The Chuck Berry Tape Massacre" first appeared in *The Carolina Quarterly*
"The Pure" first appeared in *Flypaper Lit*
"I Was There, Too" first appeared in *Vol. 1 Brooklyn*

College professors and high school and middle school teachers may order free examination copies of Seven Stories Press books. To order, visit www.sevensto-ries.com, or fax request on school letterhead to (212) 226-1411.

Printed in the USA.

9 8 7 6 5 4 3 2 1

For my father,
Gaetano Salvatore DiFrancesco,
who taught me to ask,
"What if?"

"Aw fuck it, I'm a monster, I admit it!"

—NICK CAVE, "The Curse of Millhaven"

Contents

Inside My Saffron Cave
11

A Little Procedure
27

The Disappearance
39

The Ledger of the Deep
45

The Chuck Berry Tape Massacre
59

The Pure
83

Perseus Denied
95

I Was There, Too
105

Hinkypunk
119

The Wind, the Wind
133

ACKNOWLEDGMENTS
139

Inside My Saffron Cave

for Never Angel North

Because I hated him, Mom spent the ride to Chad's house talking about Presque Isle. How lucky we would be to be so close to the state park. How fun it would be for me and her and Billy to go to the beach, ride bikes, take walks. We didn't even have bikes. We hadn't even had to rent a U-Haul to fit all our stuff into. None of it was worth taking, and Chad had promised her all sorts of things. She left so much behind, in a pile in the living room, knowing that the landlord would rather her be gone than the place be clean when she left, even. We had to leave. We had to get out before the eviction notice came to full term and followed her forever so she wouldn't even be able to rent something as bad as our old place had been. Not being barred from things was our only safety net, and she clung to it. Chad came along at the right time. With the right words. And he could even tolerate me, maybe.

But I couldn't tolerate him. And the truth was, he had so many *questions* about me, about why my mother had allowed me to do what I'd done, why I was living the way I was living, how she could support it. I turned to the back where Billy was in his car seat, drooling a little on himself as he ate a lollipop. Mom had hit her credit limit on her last card buying it, a loaf of white bread, a jar of peanut butter, and a tank of gas for the trip to Chad's house. Billy let his big sister wipe away the sticky spit from his chin, tell him lovingly how gross he is. He was only five, had only ever known me as his big sister. It'd been so easy with him. Easier than it was with Mom, even, who didn't understand but had a big enough heart to, eventually. I didn't think Chad's heart was big. I knew it wasn't. It had maybe enough room for Mom, maybe, and Billy—he was just a little boy, who couldn't love him? I was going to be the problem in the situation. I always am.

We'd lived on the lake, in a summer town. Nobody stayed past when the first blush of autumn hit the tree leaves. We'd always stayed. My mom had bartended in the summer, making the money that sometimes carried us through the winter, when she didn't drink it all away at the only place that stayed open for the locals. When she did, she picked up cleaning jobs in the winter. Back years ago, when my dad was still around, I used to break into the summer places with my friends. We didn't steal anything, we didn't break anything, we weren't those kinds of kids, the kind who just wanted to fuck with the summer people. We would break in in the winter and just hang out, sometimes smoking weed we'd stolen from our parents, even though we were only twelve or so at the time. My hair was short back then, I wore baggy boy's clothes, nobody knew, even I didn't let myself know. We used to sit in these big plush chairs, pretend the place was ours. After a while, after we got stoned or drank the beers some older kid had bought us, we'd just sit there, talking, dreaming shit up. About how we'd buy one of these places one day, no more living in the uninsulated houses that the lake effect's cold winds cut right through the walls of. When we left, we cleaned up after ourselves so no one would know we'd been there. That way, we could always go back.

My mom was still talking about Presque Isle, even though I wasn't listening and she knew I wasn't listening. Her face was drawn, it had gotten worse in the last few years. When I was younger, she had been beautiful, really stunning, with her long black hair and pale skin and bright green eyes. Her eyes had become bloodshot, and there were burst veins around her nose that you could see when she didn't wear foundation, like she wasn't then. The guys in the bar, they still got the best version of her, the one that wore the makeup and the clothes that hid her beer belly, the one who smelled like faint, summer perfume. I could see her disintegrating. I knew she thought Chad was her last hope, and that was why she was hanging on so tight, even though Chad didn't understand how she could let me be the person I am.

"You won't have to see him much, you know," she said finally, agitated that I wasn't paying her any attention. "He works so hard, such long hours. He isn't around much, and when he is, he'll mostly be with me."

Chad's the foreman of a local construction unit. We'd been to Chad's house before; he and his friends built it themselves. It's huge and the outer walls are lined with puzzle pieces of fieldstone. I saw my mom's face light up the first time he had us over for dinner. It didn't dim as Chad asked me questions that weren't really questions but hate disguised as inquisitiveness. It had been five years since I started presenting the way I felt, and I'd gotten used to discerning the reality of such things. My mom, she still didn't know.

"Well, it's only two more years until I graduate," I said. "I guess I can tolerate him that long."

"Look, we're going to have a great time out here, when I'm not working. You'll see. You'll want to go to the island every day."

"It's a peninsula," I said quietly.

She stared straight ahead, as if she could already see Chad's house and him in it, waiting for her. I spread peanut butter on a slice of bread, folded it in half, tore half off, and gave it to Billy. Then, eating the other sticky half myself, I signed on to Snapchat and began talking to my friends.

———

That night, after Chad had moved our clothes and the few other things we'd brought into the house, he and Mom got drunk in the kitchen while making dinner. Me and Billy sat playing Mario Kart Tour in the living room, on Chad's big TV. Chad said he'd bought the game for us, but he was playing it when we got there. My mom's face had lit up like she'd won the lottery when he said it, and she'd shot me a look behind her joy.

I could hear them dancing around and clinking glasses in there while old country music played on the kitchen speakers. Or something gravelly and slow. *Promise you'll find me, I want you to find me.* Billy was happy, light splashing off the screen onto his little face. There was that, at least.

"Hey, come in, come in," Mom yelled finally. The house smelled good, like onions and garlic and cream and butter. Mom's a great cook, when she doesn't pass out before dinner. I don't blame her, really I don't. She's had it hard. After my dad died, there's been a lot of things that I wouldn't wish on anybody, most of all someone like her, who gives and gives to people until she's got nothing left. But it attracts the wrong kind of people, always, all her selflessness. I've promised myself I'm never going to be like that.

Dinner was sitting out on plates when we got there, like we were some family in a sitcom. Me and Billy sat at the table, and Chad poured himself and Mom two more drinks, gin and tonic. Billy got juice and I drank water. I didn't drink anymore, ever, not after watching Mom, and I don't think Chad would've given me one anyway. They were still tipsy, walking around, grabbing forks and knives, and sharing a sloppy, drunken kiss by the sink. I turned away and looked out the window, toward the lake.

You can see the lake from Chad's house, it's right on the water. Mom told me once that, being a bachelor, not having a wife and kids, Chad had saved up a lot of his money so he could live the way he wanted to, make his house perfect. She'd told me that like a warning, almost. I got the subtext that I was not to fuck it up. I looked over the dark lake, a lake I've known all my life. It looked different from here than it did from our old summer town. As if it belonged just to the people who lived on it, while where we were from it looked as if it was for anybody. I hated this view.

Dinner tasted good, was okay, I guess. Chad kept trying to talk to me about the game that Billy and I had been playing, but I didn't say much. I kept looking at my phone. I kept refreshing Instagram and going onto my Snapchat app. Mom hates that I talk to people on the internet more than I talk to her or anybody else I know. But, honestly, when you grow up somewhere like where I grew up, the internet is the only place you can find people like you. She thinks it's all rapists and neo-Nazis, but if I didn't have my other trans friends on the internet, I wouldn't have anybody to talk to about things, ever.

I was talking to my friend Zoe, a trans woman who lives in San Francisco. I can't wait until I have a life like hers. She's older, twenty-two, and she looks out for me a lot. We were talking about how I could get estrogen, something we talked about all the time. She knew Mom wouldn't let me go on puberty blockers, and there was no doctor around here that would prescribe them, anyway.

"Put the phone away, we're having dinner," Chad said, when he realized I wasn't going to respond to him. I looked up at him. I'm not great at hiding what's inside me, it always shows up on my face. I've always been that way. Before I came out, before I started to dress and act the way I wanted to, my mom always used to take my face in her hands and ask me what was wrong, why I looked so sad, what was inside my head. I could never tell her, not then. And when I finally did, she cried and cried for about a week before she pulled herself back together and said we were going to face everything together, and that was that.

"You can't talk to me like I'm your kid," I said finally.

My mom put her fork down. Actually, she dropped it, and it made a loud noise against her plate. "June," she slurred at me.

"I'm not his daughter."

Chad cocked his head at me and lowered the shelf of his heavy eyebrows as if I was an insolent employee on one of his construction sites. "Are you anybody's?" he said, then, before Mom could realize, he added, "You don't listen to your mother, that's for sure."

But I got it. I heard the subtext. I knew what he was saying. I left the room and went to lay down in the cot he'd set up for me in one of the guest rooms. It was just until he got us some beds, he'd said.

I went on one of my gaming sites. I played some old 8-bit games, just to fuck around, to not think the thoughts in my head. My avatar on the site is the best picture of me, from a straightforward angle, my blue eyes big and my face all cheekbones. I almost look exactly how I want in it. It wasn't long before some older guy started talking to me, asking me to send him more pictures. In the dark of the room, I turned on my flash and took some more selfies at just the right angle and sent them his way.

"I'd like to take you away," he typed at me. "Marry you."

"I'm sixteen," I wrote back. And then I signed off with a sigh.

Mom was up earlier than I expected her to be the next morning. I could hear and smell bacon popping and sizzling in the kitchen, all the way from the upstairs room I was in. Mom didn't have a job yet, and I guess she wanted to make everyone as happy as she could until she got back behind a bar most of her nights again. She hadn't cooked twice in a row for me and Billy in a while.

I went into the bathroom and shaved, then wandered downstairs in my pajama pants, expecting to see only her and Billy. It was early, around eight, but I knew that Chad got up before dawn for work. But there he was, sitting at the table, waiting to be served. I noticed the gray day outside on the lake. I guess his work had been rained out for the day.

"Hey, Junie," my mom said, kissing me on the cheek as if the night before hadn't happened. She was willing everything to be okay. That's how she gets by, has gotten by for so long. No matter what happens to her, no matter what scumbag steals her tips after she let them into the house to drink or get high, no matter what guy slaps her, no matter what, my mom always tries to start a new day as if it's brand new. I'll never be like that, either.

"Morning, Mom," I mumbled. "Chad."

Billy was still sleeping, and my mom served us all breakfast without waking him up. "I'll cook again for him later," she said. That was something I hadn't seen her do, maybe ever, cook a meal at two different times. I guess her honeymoon period with Chad was spilling over on everybody.

"Maybe we'll go down to Presque Isle later if it clears up," my mom chirped at me, as we sat poking over-medium eggs with bacon strips.

"Don't want to go down there today," Chad said. "Not with the storm."

"But the rain's gotten lighter than this morning," my mom said. "It might clear by afternoon."

"Storm days, there won't be a lot of people there. Old legend. The Storm Hag."

My ears perked up and I googled "Lake Erie Storm Hag." I clicked on the images tab, and there she was, this fearsome creature with green skin, green hair, green teeth. Her eyes were without irises, black like a low storm. Jenny Greenteeth, they called her. They blamed her for the wrecks of ships, for calling sailor boys down to their watery deaths. Something vibrated in me.

Chad was still talking, but I didn't hear him, glossed over his words in my head, searching out more of this Storm Hag.

I came back to his words as he was saying to my mom, "Just a local legend. Like Bessie or those orange-eyed Bigfoots. Probably nothing. Still, you'll find a lot fewer people on Presque today than you would with clear skies."

"Good," I said. "I hate people. Mom, let's go later."

Chad glared at me, as if I was defying him again, like I had last night with the phone. I guess I was testing him. I do push things sometimes. I could have just said nothing.

When my mom picked up the plates and was at the sink rinsing them off under the loud water, Chad got up to get more coffee. He stopped by where I was sitting and said, real low, "Watch your fucking mouth around me."

I glared up at him and said, just as low, "My mother deserves better than you."

He smirked. "She's had worse."

And it was true, I knew it was true, and he knew it was true. But somehow, I don't think he meant the drinking buddies that came around only on payday, when the house was stocked with liquor, I don't think he meant the guys who hit her, I don't think he meant the stints in rehab when one of the boyfriends decided he wanted to spend her money on meth. I think he meant me. I think he meant the fights that happened at school, back when I first came out, my mom having to come in and try to explain things she didn't even understand to people who understood even less. I think he meant the looks we'd get, walking around our summer town, when she would try to hold her head high and call me the name I'd chosen. I think he meant me, and all I've put her through. And I think what he meant was that no matter what a shit-ass he was, he was *still* better than all of it, and that's all he ever had to be. Not good to her. Not good to me or Billy. Just not as bad.

"Fuck you, Chad," I said, and walked out of the room.

As I went upstairs, I googled "Jenny Greenteeth" on my phone, and I found this song that she sings, like a siren, right before she pulls the men down. "Come into the water, love, / Dance beneath the waves, / Where dwell the bones of sailor lads / Inside my saffron caves." I thought of how lonely the Storm Hag must be, underneath all that green water.

Later that day, Mom and Billy and I were standing on the shoreline, Mom with this dumb set of yellow binoculars that Chad had given her.

"It's the best time for waterfowl migration," she said. "We can see more birds here than we ever have in our lives, probably."

Mom doesn't know anything about birding. Chad must have told her, just like he gave her those dumb, glowing binoculars that Billy kept grabbing for. She would bend down and hold them up to his face, and then, after he looked and laughed, he would swat them away. She asked if I wanted to see. I said no. I didn't know what different kinds of birds were, and neither did she.

I wandered down the beach by myself while she tried to show Billy seagulls and some other birds nobody knew the names of. I kicked the sand with my bare feet. I'd taken my Chuck Taylors off, even though it was April, even though the water had made the sand cold, and my feet were cold, too. The day was still gray, but she had been right: the rain had lessened.

I kept walking the beach, even though I could hear Mom

calling for me to come back. I pretended the low waves from the earlier storm were too loud, that I couldn't hear her. I kept thinking about the next two years stretching out in front of me like the long sand of the isle. I had kept my grades up in school. I'd already applied to college, as an early-decision candidate. I wrote sad essays about my hardships. I could make it until then, I kept telling myself, just like I was walking one foot in front of the other down this beach, until I got all the way to the end.

"Love," I heard.

I snapped my head to the side, thinking my mom had come up behind me, run to catch me, whispered this soft word under her breath.

But she wasn't there. No one was at the part of the beach I was except me and the birds, diving and swooping in the stormy sky in an untethered wind dance.

We'd been at Chad's house eight days when he slapped my mother. I just sat there and watched. Billy started to cry. Chad stood back in the middle of the living room, where he'd done it, as if he was waiting for all of us to come together and attack him. None of us did anything. My mom sat down on the couch with her hand on her cheek, crying.

"Take Billy and put him to bed," she said. So I did.

I tucked his blanket that he loves, the little fuzzy baby-blue one, right up under his chin while I kept saying, "It'll be okay, it'll be okay," until he stopped crying.

"Why did he hit her?" he kept asking. "Why did Chad hurt Mommy?"

"Because Chad's an asshole," I said. "Just don't go near him. Stay away."

And I thought of my little brother stuck here all these years after I was gone. I thought of the man that Chad would try to make him into. I kept smoothing Billy's hair, promising things would be okay, when I knew it was a lie, when I knew I'd have to abandon him as soon as I could, leave him with this mess. Eventually, he believed my lies, and he went to sleep.

When I went back downstairs, Mom and Chad were drinking together in the kitchen. They had music on, and while I watched from the shadows of the living room, he took her hand and began dancing her around the kitchen. She leaned her cheek, the cheek that was still red from his hand, against his shoulder and smiled.

Mom's happy, I thought. And I slunk off to bed.

I thought about it more in bed. *Happy*. Her head on his shoulder, smiling up at him. I thought about how I would never be like that, taking just what I can get and being happy with it. I thought a lot of mean things about her and how I would never be them, while I was lying in the dark of my room on the cot. But then, then, like always, my mind turned back to the person *I* was. And I thought of all the things I wanted to be, and couldn't. My shoulders are big, I'm tall, my breasts haven't grown in yet, because I haven't been able to start HRT, and I wear these fake ones under my bra. I'm blond, as my dad was, so I don't have a ton of facial hair, but I shave first thing in the morning, and often again in the afternoon. The girls I talk to on the internet, the ones who transitioned later, call it being *poisoned by testosterone*. I thought of all the things I hated about myself, not what I hated about Mom—how many things I'm forced to be that I wish I wasn't.

That was how I fell asleep that night.

⟶

The next morning, Mom went out looking for work. Chad was already gone when I woke up, and for a minute I thought maybe it would be okay, if it was like this.

I poured myself and Billy bowls of cereal for breakfast, and then I packed up a little bag with sunblock and water, and I put Billy's hat on, and I walked us toward the bus. The bus took a long time to get to Presque Isle, about an hour, and it rumbled and rocked the whole way there. Billy was sleeping by the time we arrived, his little hands slack on my phone as it lay in his lap. I had let him play games on it. I grabbed it back and opened my apps. I had an email from Zoe. She asked whether I wanted her to send some estrogen, since I can't get it anywhere around here. She said it was how we look out for one another. We'd been talking about the risks of doing it without a doctor supervising, but after the night before, I wasn't sure I could wait anymore. I can't stand waiting. I want to be who I want to be. So I sent her an email back, asking her to send it in the mail. She wrote back immediately and said she'd do it that day.

Out on the peninsula, Billy pointed to birds, yelling *egret!* at them and chasing them down the sand.

"Who taught you that?" I said at the odd word coming out of his little-boy mouth.

"Chad!" he yelled back.

Chad.

I sat in the sand watching him, tensing up when he got too close to the water. I sat there singing some song under my breath, a song I couldn't place, something I could remember only a word of, here and there. *Water, love, dance, waves.* And a tune I could recall only bits of, here and there.

Billy ran into the water up to his knees, splashing with his feet, before I could chase after him. I screamed and ran, hoping he wouldn't get caught in some weird undertow, pulled out to the deep. I grabbed him and smacked his bottom, and he started to cry. I didn't feel bad. I felt wild and full of adrenaline.

"Do you want that Storm Hag to get you? Is that what you want?"

He cried harder, and my heart suddenly broke apart into pieces. I hugged him, little wet-legged pants and all, and we walked toward a stand where I bought him a cherry ice pop that stained his chin and tongue bright red.

———

A few days later, the box of estrogen and testosterone blockers and needles came when my mom and Chad weren't at home. I hid them in my room. When my mom got home, I grabbed my bookbag stuffed with them and a beach towel, and headed toward the bus. I told her I'd be home later.

A storm was coming in over the peninsula, low steel clouds rumbling out over Lake Erie. Nobody was there. The wind blew my hair sideways. I thought about the Storm Hag, about how cold and lonely it would be to live at the bottom of the lake. I thought about the men I talk to late at night on the internet, after I finish up talking to my trans friends online, the older ones who I know are trying to pick me up on gaming sites, like the man the other night. I thought of the Storm Hag calling up from the caves at the bottom of the lake.

I shot the estrogen into my thigh on the empty beach. When I was done, I pulled some lake water into the syringe. It was tinged green—algae, slime, who knows what. I shot it into my other leg. The song, the words *love*, *dance*, *waves*, ran through my head. Sitting in the low waves, with the sand all around me, I picked up a long piece of seaweed and twisted it into my blond hair. And another. A third. I took my compact mirror out of my bag and looked at myself. The seaweed had cast a green tint across my skin and eyes. I smiled into my reflection. My teeth emeralded back.

A Little Procedure

for Rosemary Kennedy

As I lay on the table, he said, "List the men, Lily."

I could feel the shaft of steel pressing between my eyeball and my eye socket. I knew what he meant.

There had been that brief, bright period when I was away at school, when the old nuns would fall asleep with their rosaries clutched in their hands, and I would listen to them sleep-breathe, slow and long. The stockinged feet on cold floors, the tumblers of locks clicking so loudly in the quiet. And me running through the streets, free. The men in the bars. The men with their calloused hands, lighting my cigarettes. And later, in their dirty rooms, so unlike my sterile dorm room with its starched sheets that someone came to change every morning while I went to class. Later, their calloused fingers brushing against my nipples, pushing apart the slickness of the place between my legs, against the soft skin of my inner thighs.

And so, I began to list them.

"The first one was named Marty," I said. "He was a salesman. Went from one place to the next, one woman to the next. I liked that."

"Did you, Lily." It wasn't a question.

"Yes, I did. He didn't know my family, didn't know me, never would. It was over quick. A hotel room he rented. Almost like a surgery."

The steel moved.

"And then?"

"Second was Andrew. Nice man. Married."

"Married? Oh, Lily, this is for the best."

"Married. He was like an inmaminal in bed. Very aggressive."

"The third?"

The steel moved, looser it seemed. It didn't hurt, not in the way I thought it would.

"Slewshen. A sliver a slanger a singer in a nightclub. A performer. A pring plata sang. A go a go a go."

"You'll be better soon, Lily."

And then it was darkness. And then Lily, as I knew myself, was no longer.

My father told me about the procedure only just before it was to happen. A few hours before that, he and my mother picked me up at the boarding school. They spent a long time in the office of the headmistress. Then they said we were going to lunch.

They were quite pleasant—I knew I had embarrassed them, and I wasn't sure *why* they were so pleasant. They chatted about my brothers and their accomplishments, how wonderful things were at home. I sulked a bit at that. They had sent me off because things had never been that good with me. They sent me away where the eyes that fell and fawned on my brothers wouldn't fall on me. Always behind in my studies, never able to do the things that girls my age did, to go on the dates with the young men, to have the coming-out party my mother had always dreamed of throwing for a daughter. *I'm not stupid!* I had screamed at them so often. And then, as my brothers grew, moved on to college, as my own body filled out and became older, I would scream, *I'm not a child!*

My mother and I fought and fought. As my body grew bigger, I began to fight with her physically. My father (or one of my brothers, if they were home) would grab my wrists, and my mother would cry. And then there would be the hushed voices behind Mother and Father's closed bedroom door about the scandal I would bring about, sooner or later.

They didn't mention any of this as they took me to a restaurant out near a lake, with heavy wooden doors. I never got to explore the area around my school, except the nights I snuck out, and I had no idea where we were.

We had the loveliest lunch—fresh fish, roasted vegetables, creamy mashed potatoes with just enough salt and pepper, conversation that skirted all the things that made me angry, that made them angry. We didn't talk about what my father called the family's "reputation for excellence." We didn't talk about whatever the nuns had spoken to them about. I chattered happily with them, as I hadn't in so long, about the books I was making my halting progress in, the other girls locked up in the school with me. My mother reached out, during lunch, and stroked my hair. I hadn't felt her hands smooth my hair, so soothing, in some time. I leaned back a bit in the sun that shone into the restaurant and closed my eyes.

After lunch, we did not head back to the school.

"Where are we going, Daddy?" I asked.

"Well, Lily, I guess it's time we told you. You're not going back to the school right away."

"Where am I going?"

"We've found a doctor who thinks he can help you with your . . . problems."

"What problems, Daddy? What do you *mean*?" I asked, my voice rising.

"Now, Lily," he said. "There's no reason to get upset. Just like you, to get so upset when we're trying to fix things."

"You don't have to fix anything, Daddy! I'm not a child! I can live my life on my own!"

He turned to me, scaring me as we navigated the winding road. "Really, Lily? Does running off in the night with men sound as though you're making your problems better or worse? Our family has a reputation for excellence. Your behavior is going to bring us nothing but shame."

The car swerved as my father jerked his head back toward the road.

My mother, smiling sweetly under her pillbox hat, cooed, "Don't worry, dear. It's just a little procedure. It's new, but the doctor has guaranteed us it will make everything so much better."

A little procedure. This is what they called it.

———⌒

After, there was an odd peace.

My vision was blurry, but my thoughts ran brook-clear for the first time that I could recall. They moved from one part of my mind to another like silverfish.

I had two black eyes, and they handed me wide movie-star sunglasses to wear on the way home. My mother put them on my face, round circles with black plastic frames, as I bobbed along in the back seat of the car. I was silent, not wanting to share my new mind with anyone else, not yet.

I didn't say a word as Mother and Father chatted away in the front seat. How nice it was, they said, to have their beautiful baby girl back, so sweet and silent, so much like herself before all the trouble started. How wonderful it would be to bring me back home.

"Her room is all cleaned and the maid must have put new sheets on the bed and dusted," Mother said, as if recounting things she had done herself to make me happier or more comfortable upon my reentry into their home. Outside the car window, everything was a swirl of dark and light greens, the tops of the leaves and the bottoms, circling on their branches in the wind, the stalks of grass, the mossy hills. I could smell spring, and growing. Something growing inside me.

My father turned, swerving, and looked at me. He saw my head moving like a bobble doll, my movie-star sunglasses slipping down my nose. He reached back and pushed them up gently. I didn't move a centimeter.

They must never know, I decided. They must never know, until the time I chose, what had happened inside my mind. They could accept a dumb and damaged daughter much more easily than the person I felt myself as now. Not Lily, their wild, promiscuous daughter, their disappointment, the one who would never make good. No. I was someone new entirely, and I sat there, silent.

I was their quiet Lily, their shrinking violet.

After a few weeks, I began to demurely murmur, "Yes, Mama," and, "Yes, Papa," to their questions and requests. When the answer was "no," I simply stayed silent. But the answer was mostly always "yes," because they wanted good for me, my good parents, and their Lily wanted to please them. They had shown me what good they wanted for me, yes.

I sat in my chair, at the table. I sat on the end of my bed. I sat on the couch, in our drawing room. My hands were on my lap, resting lightly over the curves of my thighs. No men would touch those thighs now, not ever again. They were just a resting place now.

The spring passed into summer, and my brothers came home from college. They did not bring the girls that often accompanied them home for weekends in the summer, not with their delicate sister in the state she was in. They reacted by not reacting, at first. Their loud voices, their laughter, their plans with Father—it all fell away into silence, staring. I smiled at them softly.

"Say, Lil," my brother Joseph said. "How's that nunnery they got you in?"

I smiled, nodded, smiled.

Soon they came to treat me like a doll, picking me up and moving me from one end of a picnic blanket spread on the lawn to another, putting me in a new chair when they needed to take mine to sit closer to Father and whisper their futures in his ear. Words like *business* and *politics* and *reputation*. Poor dear Lily, they said, it was a shame, but they gamboled through the yard like golden retrievers and were jocular at dinner and were themselves in no time. My sunny, bright brothers, who always did right, and who would never embarrass the family as I would have, if they'd let me.

In the pocket of my dress, I moved a long, slender, stolen instrument in my hand as they spoke.

Toward the end of that first summer, my brother Joseph finally brought home the woman he was seeing for dinner with the family. It was a night when James was out at a sporting event. I tilted my head and smiled when spoken to. She was beautiful, blonde, younger than him, effusive to both of my parents. And when she saw Joseph's odd sister, smiling, nodding, she smiled and nodded back.

After dinner, they left me sitting in the kitchen. I moved my spoon up and down in the puddles of melted ice cream in my cup. They all sat in the drawing room, chatting away as if they'd known one another for years. I could tell, under my parents' bright voices, they were testing her for marriage material, the way they tested them all.

After some time, my parents went upstairs. No point in spoiling Joseph's night completely. I plopped my spoon in the pool of cream over and over.

"Your sister," the blonde girl said, between rustles of clothing and wet noises. "What is *wrong* with her? Sitting there staring. Scared me half to death."

I heard the door open, heard James burst into the room like a puppy.

"Oh, gee, Joseph, you'd better not let Mom see the two of you like that!"

I nodded my head, bobbed my spoon. The black eyes had healed, long since, by then.

One day the boys took me along to a picnic with their girlfriends. They had stopped looking at me. They led me out of the car, spread a checkered blanket, and sat me down on it. They disappeared in the woods and their girlfriends came back blushing. I was wearing my movie-star glasses again. I thought of my body beneath the pink and white dress I had on, one that had checks, like the blanket. I ran my hand up my thigh, remembering the men. I stopped myself from brushing against my nipple when I saw the blonde, Mary Jean, watching me.

The boys began throwing a ball back and forth. The brunette, James's girlfriend, joined in with them, as if she was one of them. I felt bad for her then, I did.

Mary Jean laughed and watched. She leaned back and looked at me. I looked ahead, silent. My nipples were hard against my bra, under my pink-and-white checked dress.

"You can do whatever you want, if it's with boys like your brothers," Mary Jean whispered to me. She didn't say it cruelly, but it was too late for kindness. "You just picked them wrong, girl."

Years passed. The boys came home less frequently, going on ski vacations and spending summers abroad. Joseph married Mary Jean, and I was a silent, retiring presence in a bridesmaid's dress at their wedding. James got into politics, in a small but powerful fashion at first, which grew as time went on. Mother and Father managed their dear Lily, rarely taking me anywhere when they realized that my silence would not break.

Sometimes Mother would drink a martini and cry.

"What did we do to her?" she would ask Father, swirling the olive-juice-clouded liquor in her V-shaped glass, her makeup running.

"We did what was best for the boys, for the family," Father would say, firmly. It became less firm as the years passed, softening like the skin under his jaw and on his forehead.

"Look at James's career," Father added.

"The boys," Mother would murmur. Her face relaxing as the liquor worked its way into her blood. "Such good boys."

⁓

In bed at night, I would run the cool metal head of the instrument between my thighs, against the slickness between my legs.

⁓

Mother drank more, and Father stayed out later. The boys were his pride, and when he was home, he spoke of them endlessly. Mother cried to me then, her silent daughter. It was a man's world, she said, and she was so sorry. I put my hand up on her cheek, but did not say a word.

In the end, Father's precious boys did not create a scandal. Neither did his dear, silent Lily. Lily who had once run so wild and free, with so many men, in the dark of night, after they sent her away for being so simple and so unrestrained, so guileless compared with her brothers, so without their charm or instincts for what was good for the family. No, the Lily who could have done such a thing was no more. And quiet, nodding Lily did nothing but finger the long instrument she had stolen from the doctor's office, all those years ago.

No, it was Father who created the scandal.

Mother drank and Father stayed out. And Father drank. And Father found a new model, one with a tight ass and a tight pussy, younger than Mother was, not that he would ever replace her, but a few words to that effect while inside this new woman wouldn't hurt anyone in the long run. Except it did. It got into the new model's head so deep that she grabbed the steering wheel when they were driving, tipsy, on a bridge, and the car went over the rail, and Father got out and the new model got sent back to the dealership, so to speak; she died on impact with the water.

Father came home that night, having walked all that way, before the cops found the crashed car, before the scandal hit. He came in the door with his disheveled shirt still marked with her lipstick and his jacket marked with his own blood.

His dear Lily sat on the couch. Sat and sat, as she had done for years. As I had done. Lily was gone. I was not.

He staggered in the door and he put his head on my lap. Dear Lily, he wept. What had he done? Was this the action of a man whose family had a reputation for excellence? No, certainly not. Certainly not.

He was in no position to think clearly. And so I lifted my hand and stroked his head. I could hear Mother weeping upstairs, as she did most nights. I stroked his hair, pushing it back from his forehead. The scandal. A little procedure to avoid so much scandal.

As he cried in my lap, I took the long, thin instrument out

of the pocket of my robe. I was no expert. In fact, there was no such thing as a lobotomist, not anymore.

No, I was not an expert. But some connections are delicate and easily severed.

I pushed the ice pick in deep.

The Disappearance

for Bob Hicok

It wasn't until Dr. Allen posted his long missive to a minor poetry magazine that Kaj began to notice how opaque he was. How he walked through the hallways that he had once borne such a presence in as if he were slowly fading from them. And, truth be told, some days it looked as if he actually was. There was a flicker of static around his edges, an indistinctness to the peach-colored line of his face, a nebulousness to his salt-and-pepper beard. Sometimes he flickered away as if the halls of the English department's offices were swallowing him whole.

The poetry magazine that the missive appeared in was one that could never have dreamed of publishing Dr. Allen, prize-winning poet that he was, years ago. But his opportunities had grown leaner, the internet and its bevies of upstarts who cared little for his distinguished prizes had grown more robust. And, despite its almost pedestrian platform, the missive caused a major stir.

Dr. Allen, it seemed, was disappearing. Or, as he wrote in the magazine, he was being disappeared.

The long screed in the minor magazine began as a typical autumn piece, the decline of a poet, a man watching a new wave crest as his own crashed to shore. But then, slowly, it dawned over the piece that the disappearance was not a metaphor. Then Dr. Allen began to point fingers.

Though Kaj was himself too minor a writer to be named in the litany of poets Dr. Allen pointed his fading finger at, he couldn't help but feel implicated. Dr. Allen's targets (or, in the logic of the screed, the people he felt were targeting him) were a group of rising star poets, Ruth Lilly Award winners, bestsellers, people who were becoming household names (even as poets). Kaj himself had been published in only a few magazines, and though they were print, though they had a solid reputation, he did not flatter himself that he was among Dr. Allen's list of perpetrators. They all had one thing in common though, those criminals of the poetry world, something that even Kaj, a lowly adjunct with a short CV, shared with them. They were all minorities.

Kaj loathed the word *minority*, but there was no other blanket term that encompassed all Dr. Allen's alleged tormentors. There was a gay Chinese man. A Black woman. A white transgender woman. The way Dr. Allen spoke of these people in his screed, they were growing as he shrank, crowding the hallways of his beloved academia with words and concepts and bodies he didn't understand—he, who had once been at the forefront of progressivism, who had protested the Kent State massacre, who had cheered on Dr. King's dream. So was the way, he had lamented in the piece—Bob Dylan had once told him, even—but did they have to make him disappear? Weren't they content to let him fade?

The day the essay came out, Kaj was alerted to it by an outraged Poetry Twitter as he sat in the adjunct lounge. Several other adjuncts were there, some of them finishing lesson plans, some of them putting on heavier makeup than they'd worn in the classroom for their upcoming bartending shifts. Kaj followed the responses from the people indicted in the piece, feeling a surge of joy and vindication that they had this space to reply in—until he realized that Dr. Allen was not and would never be on Twitter to see these responses.

When Kaj left the adjunct office and walked into the department's hallways, however, he knew he wasn't the only one to have read the essay. The tenured professors stood together, talking quietly, shaken, until Dr. Allen appeared in the hall. The crowds of English professors quieted and dispersed. There he was, the National Endowment for the Arts award-winning, much-laureled poet and professor whom droves of people had cited in their reasons for attending the university, the poet who had rubbed elbows with Robert Lowell and John Berryman and Ted Hughes. There he walked, head high, book under his arm, with his edges blurred and eroded, a hole of blankness in his forearm, beneath his short sleeves. One of the women professors gasped when she saw it, then smiled.

⟶

Kaj had a comp class to teach that afternoon. He loathed it almost as much as he hated the word *minority*, but with his student-loan repayment due every month and little else coming his way, he took the classes he could get. He wanted to teach poetry. They all wanted to teach poetry.

The students weren't bad, mostly eager to please him or so checked out they didn't cause any problems. He passed them if they put in the bare minimum of effort. They were often first-generation students, and many of them had bigger worries than his comp class. There were even a few students who loved writing in the class. They were a rarity, and the reason he'd begun teaching in the first place.

He used memes in his lesson plans to make a point that day, a cheap trick to prove he wasn't as old and removed from their lives as, say, Dr. Allen. Cheap as the ploy was, it worked. The students engaged with the lesson—even the ones who usually sat as quiet and clench-jawed as unwilling roller-coaster riders.

After class, as Kaj was putting his papers and books in his bag, he noticed one of the students lingering. She was a tiny, pale young woman, short-haired, with bitten nails, mostly quiet. She stood near the front of the room, shifting weight from one foot to the other. He struggled to remember her name and pulled "Katie" from the depths of his end-of-the-semester brain.

When the rest of the students had left the room and she remained, he said, "Hey, Katie. Did you need something?"

"Um," she said. "I guess it's not important."

She shrugged. Kaj, not knowing what else to do, shrugged back. She walked out of the room.

⟶

The next day, half of Dr. Allen's arm was gone. A slightly younger man, a tenured professor, carried his books for him.

On Thursday, after class, Katie was in front of Kaj's desk again.

"Uh, professor? Can I ask you a question?"

"About the assignment?" Kaj asked.

"No, uh. About how you knew? How did you know . . ."

Kaj put all his books back down on the desk. The campus was large, with a varied student body, and the pro-gun, right-wing students had made him hyperaware of what dangerous territory he was in at that moment. He just wanted to live his life, really. And here was Katie, asking him this. Maybe she didn't have anyone else to ask.

He held her eye. "Katie, there was never a question for me. Some things you just know."

She shifted her weight, adjusted her shoulder bag.

"Thanks," she said, and ran.

The next morning, there were two emails in Kaj's school inbox. One was from Katie. It detailed, in hurried, unpunctuated prose, a fight she had gotten into on the internet with someone who had called her a typical white cis-woman feminist—which she wasn't, she wasn't, she would like to change her name and pronouns with the school and how did one do such a thing? The second email was from the office of disability, requesting accommodations for Katie, who had been hospitalized.

Kaj was tense that day in the adjunct lounge, thinking of how he might have helped his student more. Thinking of how afraid he had become to lose his job, to do the things he had entered academia to do. He shared the lounge with a few other part-time teachers, as usual. They looked mostly frazzled, overwhelmed. He supposed he did, too.

When Kaj walked out into the hallway that day, more of Dr. Allen was gone. Kaj, who usually carried a metal straw with him, withdrew it from his bag. He didn't know why. He didn't know what he was doing. But as Dr. Allen floated, one-legged, past him in the hall, his fellow old-man professor carrying his life's work beside him, Kaj turned and put the straw in his mouth and began sucking up the air around Dr. Allen. The air whooshed toward him like a solid thing. He sucked and he spit, sucked and spit, and soon pieces of leather-elbowed jacket were coming through his straw, being spit out; bits of salt-and-pepper beard stuck to his lips. And when he was done sucking and spitting, there was an empty space in the hall where Dr. Allen had been.

The next week, Kaj received an email from the campus's registration office informing him of the name change of one of his students. Katie was now Kamron and used they/them pronouns.

Kaj was happy to see Kamron in the back of the room, as quiet as ever, their short hair cut in a distinctly more barber shop than beauty salon cut way. After class, Kaj lingered, and Kamron walked by his desk slowly, eyes down.

"That's a great new haircut, Kamron," Kaj said.

Kamron looked up and beamed before running out the door, into the hallways, leaving nothing but empty space behind them.

The Ledger of the Deep

for Sawyer Lovett

There was a memory at the heart of who he was. He was around five years old, and his father picked him up and took him through the front door, out into the yard, over to the side of the house. Where there had been a rusted muscle car and the newer car his father and mother drove, there was now a boat. It loomed in his memory, even though it was a small motorboat that could fit two or three people at most. In his mind it was huge. It rivaled the whales he had seen in picture books and on TV. He couldn't read or write, not quite, not yet, but he could make out the big block letters on the back of the boat. They were the same letters his mom and dad helped him trace and identify, the ones that spelled out his name, who he was.

"Named after you!" his dad said, bouncing him and making him laugh and smile.

This huge, wondrous thing. This whale-thing that made his father and mother laugh and break a bottle of champagne right above the name, right there in the yard, even though they got mad when he broke things made of glass. This was different—a celebration, happiness with his name on it.

He had known, in that moment, more than in any other one, how much he was loved.

———⟶

"What do you mean, you're changing your name?" his father asked. "What's wrong with Sara?"

"Dad, nothing's wrong with it, it isn't that," Sawyer said. His voice was noticeably deeper than it had been the last time he came to visit, over spring break. He thought his shoulders were broader, too, though that may have been the upper-body workouts and not the testosterone he had started taking just a few months before.

It was July, well into summer vacation. He had put off coming out here long enough, even though his dad had called several times to see when he was coming in, when they could take the boat out onto Lake Erie as they had every summer for the last fifteen years. For weeks, Sawyer had put off traveling from Clarion, where he went to school, to the tiny town on Lake Erie in Ohio that he'd grown up in. He had school, then, when school was over, he had work, then, when his father said he had to have *some* weekends off, he'd claimed to want to spend time with his partner. Because he knew it was inevitable. He knew that he would have to come out a second time to his dad, not as a lesbian, as he had two years ago, but as a trans man. And he wasn't sure his dad was ready.

His dad wasn't ready.

Sawyer felt settled into his identity. He'd been to support groups for a year. He'd had a therapist, who specialized in queer identities, for even longer. Now, standing there in front of his dad, in the driveway, where he'd thrown out the new information like a softball the minute his dad came over to hug him, he knew that he shouldn't have come.

"It's bad luck to change a name," his dad said. "Old sailing superstition. You can't just *change it*, not without the proper christening, not just like that—the gods of the sea think you're trying to deceive them, and it's bad luck. You want bad luck, Sara?"

Sawyer knew they were not talking about what they were talking about. And so the word "deceive" hit him like a punch in the stomach, like a right-wing ad for bathroom predators.

"I knew I shouldn't have told you," Sawyer muttered.

"I named the boat after you!" his father said. "What am I supposed to do, change it to a man's name?"

Sawyer got in his car and drove back to Clarion. The air conditioner in the car didn't work, and he could feel the sweat pooling under his binder above the heat of the summer highway. Back in Clarion—home—he would feel safe. It was a shitty college town, yes, but there he would have his partner, Lisa, who had supported him since day one. He would have his trans-guy gym buddies, and he would have his trans-woman friends, who called him on his shit when he got too wrapped up in playing gender games he didn't even believe in. Mostly he would not have to be around his dad.

He hit the turn signal and passed a slow-moving car, gritting his teeth, ready to be home *right then*. His dad meant well, he knew that. His dad had had a moment or two when Sawyer had come out as queer, but he'd gotten over it rather quickly. His sincere questions (*Can I still walk you down the aisle when you get married? It's not because your mother died when you were so young, is it?*) were both rankling and endearing to Sawyer. His dad didn't understand, he'd hardly left their small Ohio town. But he *wanted* to understand. He wanted to be a good father.

As Sawyer pressed down on the accelerator in increments, taking the car a bit past the point where it shook and a bit above the speed limit, he wondered whether this would be his dad's limit. Would he finally not be able to accept any more? Would this be too much to tell his buddies down at the bar he went to for a few beers every now and then? His coworkers at UPS? Sawyer's community was full of horror stories about families who abandoned their trans members. Was he going to be one of the sad queers hanging around campus on holidays like Thanksgiving when everyone else went home?

Sawyer was broken from his thoughts by the blaring of a siren behind him. As he slid his foot over to the break, he realized he'd been going at least twenty miles over the speed limit.

———

"A speeding ticket?" Lisa said when he got home. "S, you know we can't afford that. We can barely afford rent since the college crowd's gone and your job isn't as busy."

Lisa was the only one who called him S. They had been together for three years, and it had been a change for her. She had had to take gradual steps. She called him Sawyer occasionally, and slipped and called him Sara once or twice, but mostly it was S. She was pacing back and forth in front of him, raking her hand through her short black hair. Her heavy black eye makeup was beginning to smear from the tears collecting at the corners of her eyes, which she kept trying to push away.

Her worries about money weren't unfounded. Sawyer was a server at a local restaurant, and he'd told her that the blow his paycheck had taken lately was mostly from the summer break. Which wasn't untrue. But it had also coincided with when he started binding at work, when his first few chin hairs sprang up and he didn't shave them. Newly bearded, ambiguously gendered people just didn't get tipped as much as cute girls, he supposed.

"I'll figure something out, Lisa," he said. He tried to kiss the top of her head, but she slid under his hands and stood back, angry.

"We just can't afford this," she said. "Why didn't you try explaining to him why you were so upset that you were speeding?"

"Oh, yeah," Sawyer said, sarcasm creeping into his tone. "'Officer, I'm hoping you'll take my being transgender better than my father just did…' Sounds like a solid plan."

"Well, what are we supposed to do to pay it?" Lisa asked.

"It's not that big a deal," Sawyer said. "I'll pay it off in increments. It's not like we're not going to be broke for a long while, Lise."

"Things will pick up in the fall when class starts again," Lisa said. Her own job at a pet-food store paid even less than Sawyer's job. He'd been supporting both of them, really. Neither of their families was the kind that could pay their rent or send them much in the way of money.

"That's not what I mean—doctor's visits, eventually top

surgery, this is all going to cost a lot of money, Lisa," he said. "Things aren't just going to turn around immediately."

Lisa cocked her head at him. "Top surgery? I didn't know you were thinking of that. You didn't tell me."

"It's just a thought, we don't have to talk about it now," Sawyer said. "It's probably better we don't."

Lisa walked into the other room and lowered herself to the couch. "Everything's changing so much," she said.

Sawyer walked in and sat down next to her. "For both of us. It'll be okay."

She finally let him kiss her on the top of her head.

———⟶

Their friend Ellen came over that night to watch TV with them. They were in the middle of bingeing the original two seasons of *Twin Peaks* before the reboot came out. The three of them watched it only when they were together.

Sawyer made them dinner—before he'd left his father's house, his dad had raced to throw a cooler in the back of the car. Whole rainbow trout. Sawyer knew, from years on Lake Erie on his dad's boat, how to gut and debone them. His mom had taught him how to stuff them with cherry tomatoes, serrano peppers, olive oil, garlic, and herbs. She'd been gone for years now, and every time he made this dinner for the people he loved he thought of her. Thinking about his dad right now, that was a little too hard.

They ate sloppily, with olive oil on their fingers and at the corners of their mouths. They snuggled on the couch together, all three of them, watching the old weird television show, chatting and making jokes.

This was home, Sawyer thought again. He and Lisa had met Ellen in the school's LGBTQ+ club their first semester. They'd been close friends ever since, even though he and Lisa had paired off before too long. Ellen was tall and had long, dirty-blond hair, wore chunky-heeled nineties shoes, flannels, and slouchy beanies. She had a raspy voice and a dry laugh. She was one of their best friends, someone he could trust with anything.

"My dad didn't react so well," Sawyer said, when they shut the show off for the night.

"That was today?" Ellen asked. "What happened?"

"Started blabbering about how you had to be careful changing ships' names, because you don't want the sea gods to think you're 'deceptive,'" he said, shaking his head.

"No," Ellen gasped.

"Yeah. He didn't even know what he was saying."

"Well, you have us," Ellen said. She snaked her arms behind each of them on the couch, at their lower backs.

"I know," Sawyer said, snuggling close to her, as Lisa did on her other side.

"Woah, you smell totally different!" Ellen exclaimed.

"Huh?"

"I guess I haven't hugged you in a while," Ellen said. "You smell like a dude."

"Well, I am one," Sawyer said. He was trying to hold back a smile.

"I . . . I know!" Ellen stammered. "I just wasn't expecting—"

"It's okay," Sawyer said. His smile was much larger now, not a quiver at the edges but a full-fledged grin. He looked over at Lisa, who was not smiling. Who did not look very happy at all.

Lisa came into Sawyer's work a few nights later and sat at the bar. She did this sometimes, keeping him company in the lull between customers. The owners, the bartender, the other servers, and even the dishwasher all knew her and loved her. They asked Sawyer all the time when he was going to marry her.

There was a new cook, and things were coming out of the kitchen far too slow for how few guests they had. The people at the tables kept looking up, away from each other, their drinks, and their phones, and stared at all the empty seats around them. Sawyer kept trying to explain, and people kept cutting him off.

"I'm so sorry, but—"

"When will our food be here? We ordered the fish special forever ago."

Sawyer went into the back to talk to the new cook. He was in the cooler, grabbing something for the line.

"Hey, buddy, you gotta speed things up, people are getting upset," Sawyer said.

The new guy had a huge grin, too big to be real, unnerving instead of reassuring.

"Yeah, boss, I'm on it," he said. "Hey—that your sister out there? With all the eye makeup?"

Sawyer laughed, leaning into the cooler. "No, my girlfriend."

"Lemme ask you," the new guy said, "you're the one with the dick, right?"

"Excuse me?"

"I mean, now don't get upset, boss, I'm just—I know how it works."

"Fuck you," Sawyer said, coming out of the cooler and

closing the door behind him. He shook his head and walked to the front.

"You will never believe what this douchebag said to me," he muttered to Lisa as he walked by the bar. "I'll tell you tonight."

Lisa stayed around as they closed up, helping Sawyer put chairs up on tables and sweep underneath them. When everyone had left but them, when they were alone smoking outside, on their way to their cars, Lisa said, "You know, maybe if you just didn't wear your binder to work, you'd make the money you used to."

"Fuck, Lisa, not tonight, okay?"

They drove home and went to bed without saying another word.

⸻

Sawyer's dad kept calling. Sawyer didn't answer, but his dad left voicemails.

"Hey, Sar— Sawyer," he'd say. "I wanted to talk to you about something. I'm sorry about the name thing. But this renaming thing—I know it's superstition, but it's just not good luck. Call me, I want to talk to you about it."

"Hey, Sa . . . wyer. Give me a call. We'll take the boat out, summer's almost over. Get your ass back here."

It went on for weeks. Sawyer could never call back.

⸻

One night, he and Lisa were lying in bed after sex when Lisa ran her hand over his chest.

"Don't, you'll stick to me," he joked. "It's so hot, and we're both covered in sweat."

A breeze was blowing in the window of their tiny bedroom. They lived in a space only really meant for one. There was a tiny bedroom, a lofted bed, a work desk underneath it, a tiny living room, and a minuscule kitchen where they cut vegetables and meat on top of the stove. It had always seemed like enough, but lately it had seemed too small for both of them, too hot, too close. Now the space between them on the bed seemed enormous, too big to possibly fit in the space of the bedroom. Until Lisa closed it, running her hand over his chest.

"What, I can't touch you there anymore?" Lisa said. "You used to like it."

"I never liked it," Sawyer said. "I just didn't feel anything."

"Are you really going to have top surgery one day? We never talked about it."

"I don't know, Lisa," he said. "I'd like to. When I picture myself, I don't have breasts."

He didn't notice for a few minutes that Lisa was crying.

"What's wrong?"

"It's too much, S," she said. "First your name, then your pronouns, soon your body. I want to be supportive. But I'm a goddamn lesbian, S, I *like* tits. I like women. I like people with curves and soft bodies, who smell like girls ..."

"Are you telling me you don't like the way I smell?" Sawyer said. It seemed like an appalling thing to say to your partner, albeit one hundred percent reasonable. His entire body had changed. Of course he didn't want her to pretend that wasn't the case.

"I miss Sara," she said, crying.

There was nothing Sawyer could say.

He did not get a speeding ticket on the way back home, even though he drove as fast as he had driven away from there the last time. He didn't call his father, either. He showed up at the door, in the early hours of a late-summer night. The sky was twilight and magical over the lake, shades of pastel and dusk.

"Sawyer!" his dad said, opening the door. He was in his boxers and a T-shirt, carrying a can of beer. Sawyer thought, not for the first time, but for the first time in a long time, of how sad his dad's life was here now, alone. He'd never made a lot of friends. He hadn't dated since Sawyer's mom died. And with Sawyer gone, it was just him.

It took Sawyer a minute to realize his dad hadn't stumbled over his name.

Before he knew it, his dad was fully dressed, and not long after that they were pulling into the dock, and then they were on the water. The boat *SARA* motored out to the deeper waters, where they drifted, watching the stars wink into the sky.

"What happened?" his dad asked. He was not an unkind man, not an unperceptive one. His life hadn't given him opportunities, but he hadn't been unhappy, either.

"Lisa," Sawyer said. They moved to the front of the boat, where they sat facing each other. Sawyer's dad opened a cooler he'd brought, handing Sawyer a beer.

"Broke up with you?"

"Um-hm."

They sat in silence for a while.

"You know why it's bad luck to rename a boat?" his dad asked.

"Yeah," Sawyer said, trying not to cry. "Deception of Poseidon. Got it."

"Every boat's name is written in the Ledger of the Deep. You can't just change it. You remember the old story about the *Admiral?* The tug that was renamed and went down in Lake Erie?"

"Yeah, there was some stuff about a clairvoyant who had a seizure just before it happened."

"Ship hand. Replaced on board by a Gypsy who played the fiddle in storms," his father said.

"Dad." Sawyer frowned.

"Oh, right, what's the word? Romani?"

"Yeah, Dad."

"Anyway, the ship went down and the Romani guy was playing his violin in the middle of it, and you can still hear the violin on the lake some nights. All because they renamed a boat and forgot to ask the blessing of Poseidon. Bad luck."

"Yeah, thanks for really hammering it home, Dad," Sawyer said. He threw his can over the side of the boat, wishing he'd never come back.

"Sawyer, I want to tell you, I spent the last six weeks trying to figure out how to rename a boat."

Sawyer looked at him.

"You have to scrub every trace of it—in every ledger, in every place it's ever been written. Then there's a big invocation of the gods of the sea and wind and all this business. That's so your luck stays okay."

"But you didn't do it," Sawyer said.

"No, I didn't. I started to do it, then I thought I might better spend my time by reading that gay website you told me about a while back, what's it, HAPPY?"

"GLAAD, Dad."

"Yeah. And PFLAG and all that. So I did that for a while. And I'm sorry I ever said anything about deception, and I guess . . . were you trying to tell me . . . ?"

"Yeah, Dad."

"Anyway, that's when I decided the boat's name is Sawyer now."

"But you didn't change it." Sawyer laughed. "I saw the name when we got in."

"Yeah, well, that's what we're calling it now. To hell with the sea gods. We make our own goddamn luck. We always have."

Sawyer's dad's face went still in the gathering darkness. He seemed to be listening hard for something in the distance.

"Do you hear music?" he said finally.

"No," Sawyer said, straining. He sat for a few minutes before he realized his dad had been messing with him.

"Of course there's no goddamn violin," his father said, hysterical. "Give me another beer, son."

The Chuck Berry Tape Massacre

for Jeff Mangum

The news was on the TV. The news flashed in red and yellow. The news was danger. Danger was on the TV screen. The news asked again and again, Will your world end?

Kay's daughters lay on the carpet on either side of her. She had barely roused them from sleep; they were still tangled in blankets and teddy bears and elastic-banded pajama shorts. Kay cooed soothingly at them, even as the orbs of her eyes remained fixed on the yellow and red letters on the dangerous screen.

As the news flashed, Kay brought her left thumb up to her lips and drew the sign of the cross. She kissed the daughter to her left on the forehead. She brought her right thumb up to her lips, made the same talismanic motion, and kissed the arch of the foot of the daughter to the right. The daughters squirmed a bit under this unexpected attention but remained otherwise enmeshed in the strands of sleep.

Meltdown. So close by. Kay could remember pictures of Hiroshima, Nagasaki. Skin melting. Legs running. She could hear the wail of sirens—were they in the streets or on the screen? She wanted to scream but could not. The girls had only her. She had to be strong.

They had been alone like this, the three of them, for so long. Her husband had disappeared one day. Her mother and father had died. Alone with the two girls, Kay took her role as protector in great earnestness. Each night, as the girls went to bed, she kissed her thumb and dragged two perpendicular lines across the lock on their door. A cross. A talisman. Kay's protection.

Now, shaking in the night, Kay wrapped first the girl to her left, then the girl to her right, methodically in their blankets. She picked up the youngest as if she were two instead of five and tucked the bottom corner of the blanket up over her feet. Then Kay folded either corner over the girl's torso, and finally the top triangle of cloth down over her head. Kay then wrapped the awkward, limp bundle in her arms and drew it toward her chest. The girl's head and feet drooped down where her mother could not support them. Kay then put down the youngest daughter and repeated the process more awkwardly still with the sleeping seven-year-old.

Kay packed the girls into the back seat of the long, hearse-like black four-door her husband had left behind. On summer days when the car wouldn't start and Kay had to walk to work, the girls used the interior expanse of tan plush as a hiding spot in games of hide-and-seek. One would sprawl her sweaty limbs (made sweatier by the rising heat inside the car) across the back seat or the floor, hoping the other could not rise far enough on her toes to see her there as she peeked through the window.

Now that same tan plush cradled the wool blankets that made their warm nighttime cocoons. They rocked rhythmically with each hitch in the engine. Each imperfect hiccup of the transmission helped spiral them deeper into their dreams.

"Everything will be fine, fine, fine," Kay chanted, pulling the massive car around a wide arc. The girls felt vaguely as if they would keep going, keep turning, launch up, off, out into space.

Kay drove in a circle around the town. In the back, the girls opened their wide drowsy black eyes every now and then, blinked wetly. As the hours of the night stretched on, the circles Kay moved in became smaller and tighter. They finally came to rest back in the driveway of their own home, the engine of the car clicking as it cooled, heat cascading off the hood into the warm fall night.

Disaster. Disaster. Disaster disaster disaster. Will your world end?

Kay drew a breath from the dark air and lifted her daughters to her chest.

The school nurse sat behind the desk in her office, not one white hair in her old-fashioned updo out of place. To the left of her desk was a line of plastic chairs. This was where the children sat and waited for her to lead them off to the small room to the right of her desk—the examination room. In the examination room, there were two small cots separated by a paper curtain. Straight across from the nurse's desk was a metal door painted a noncommittal sky blue on both sides. It was this door that burst open as if there were a fire on the other side of it. Kay came through it, her arms loaded with clothes, tendrils of hair flying wildly around her face like snakes around a Medusa's head.

"Where is my daughter?" she hissed at the nurse. She paused after every word.

"Mrs.—"

"Where is she?" Kay demanded.

The nurse had dealt with upset parents for years, but found herself frozen before Kay. How strange. There was nothing imposing or even significant about this woman. And still the nurse felt her well-crafted superiority crumble. She smoothed her hair into place, though it was already perfect. Still losing the struggle to find words, the nurse pointed Kay toward the examination room.

Kay shot through the door, making the paper curtain billow and crinkle. She dropped the armful of clothes on the cot and gathered up her youngest daughter in both arms. The room was perfumed with the sickening odor of rotten flowers and garbage.

"Mama," said Kay's youngest daughter, cuddling to her mother's chest.

"Oh, Baby," said Kay. It was as if the odor assailing her nostrils did not exist. Nothing existed except her daughter, whom she would protect, whom she would care for. The child wept against her mother's chest for a moment. Then, when the tears stopped, Kay picked up the clothes she had brought and gave them to the child. The little girl disappeared into the bathroom.

The nurse had appeared in the doorway while Kay held her daughter. As soon as the little girl was safely behind the door, Kay's face contorted from a look of comfort to one of rage.

"What have you people done to her?" she hissed.

"Excuse me? You don't mean—"

"Don't you *tell me*," Kay continued, her mouth twisting like the body of an injured snake, "that a healthy child just shits in her pants in class and *sits in it* for an hour without saying anything. Do *not* try to tell me that."

The nurse moved her mouth around words that made no sound, spittle flying from her lips. "Children have accidents!" she finally managed. "These things happen all the time. No one has done anything to your daughter, unless you consider your—"

At that moment, the little girl emerged from the bathroom in the sweatpants and sweatshirt Kay had brought her. Kay's face softened, and the nurse would later say that she could hardly believe the woman who confronted her was the same woman who so tenderly drew her small daughter into her arms.

"There is something wrong with this school," Kay said. Her words were sharp, while the hands that smoothed wisps of the child's hair from her face were beyond soft. "Don't expect to see my daughters here again."

Kay's oldest daughter's class was studying Native Americans and had built a tepee in their classroom. A real tepee would have been made of thick branches and animal hide. Theirs was made of thick cardboard poles and brown paper. The teacher had done most of the construction. The children had painted the outside with symbols that meant nothing to anyone but them, that didn't go higher than three feet from the ground.

Kay's oldest daughter sat inside the tepee. It seemed to go up forever, tapering, ending in a little hole. The paper around her crinkled as she breathed. It was cool and smooth and the brown of a fawn. The children were allowed twenty minutes in the tepee each day, to do as they wished, as long as they did it quietly.

Kay's oldest daughter was inside the tepee with her math homework sitting in front of her. She stared at the page. In her mind there were steady sounds. Scales. Plink plink plink plink—plink plank plank plunk.

The sounds she could almost hear rose above her, out the hole in the top of the tepee, like smoke. She prodded a mole on the back of her left hand with her finger, wondering if it was cancer. She didn't feel particularly convinced it was, or it was not. She let this thought, too, drift away and out. Her breath was so natural it almost did not exist. She didn't have many moments like this, alone.

The paper of the tepee rustled as the classroom door opened. Kay came in, her youngest daughter slung on her hip, the little girl blinking and sucking her thumb. The children and the teacher all grew quiet as Kay called her oldest daughter's name.

Kay's oldest daughter came out of the tepee holding her math book in front of her stomach. Her eyes didn't meet anything, as if she had been caught doing something shameful.

"Come with me now," Kay said. She held her hand straight out. The line of her commanding arm seemed to cut directly through the rabble of seven-year-old heads. Her daughter bowed her head and swayed closer to her. She dropped her math book on the floor. It fell in a catastrophic rustle. Pages detached and flew ways they should not have, like broken birds from a nest.

When the door of the classroom slammed again, it was the last anyone in the school saw of Kay's daughters.

Kay went through the proper channels, sent the right letters. The girls were officially withdrawn from school. The girls were to be homeschooled.

But their problems were not over. There were bad gases in the basement. Kay was not sure which. Radon? Freon? She could feel them sliding up the stairs, pushing up through the floorboards. The girls' toys and games were in the basement. They could not understand why Kay would not let them down there, and she could not tell them.

"But, Mom!"

"But, Mom!"

"You will stay on this floor! You will not go near the stairs!"

Then the upstairs began to shrink. Kay could see the gases in the kitchen. One day, during dinner, she saw them swirling, black and green, above the plates of food. She moved cans of food and plates and boxes into the living room, hung curtains in the kitchen doorway and tacked them down at the edges. Then the living room was cordoned off. Finally, Kay's master bedroom and bathroom became living room, kitchen, schoolroom, and bedroom to her and the girls. Kay piled cans along the walls, brought in bottled water that she kept near the cans. She installed a padlock on the door herself and wore a key around her neck.

The dull metal of the cans gleamed with light refracted off the bottles of water. Down the middle of the room ran a curtain. On either side of the curtain sat an old-fashioned wooden chair with a desk attached to it. In the chairs, the girls sat with notebooks and pencils before them, waiting for their lessons.

"Music lesson! Are you ready?"

"Yes, Mom."

"It's Ms. Mercer! Your music teacher's name is Ms. Mercer!"

"Yes, Ms. Mercer!"

"Scales." Plink plink plink plink—plink plank plank plunk. "Now you."

Plink plink plink plink—plink plank plank plunk.

"Very good!"

"Thanks, Mom!"

"It's Ms. Mercer when I teach you music!"

"I mean, thanks, Ms. Mercer!"

Late at night, the bed we all sleep in begins to suffocate me. There's enough room. The sheets are soft and smell like rain. But I'm choking. I can't breathe. I slide over the side. I pull the toy piano and the tape recorder we use for music lessons into the bathroom.

The shower stall is white, but turning gray and black from slimy stuff growing on the walls. The slimy stuff starts in the corners and clumps its way up and around. I lie flat out in the shower, flat out on my back.

I remember old radio shows. My mommy says I can't really remember my daddy, but I can. I remember listening to the radio with him and my mommy late at night. I was little, but I can remember music and red and green lights coming out of the radio and my mommy and daddy's faces and cars running by on the summery street crushing rocks underneath their wheels. I lie on the white and the black and the gray shower floor and I open my throat as wide as I can and feel summer nights and radio and red and green lights and love and no more sadness in it. I don't know how to sing, but somehow I sing and I sing and I sing.

And I am not where I am anymore.

People come in to sell bootleg tapes, old albums, movies. Some are collectors, who always seem to wear strange, outdated clothes that smell like mothballs, or who sweat too much from the hands as they give me whatever they're selling. Collectors are the strangest people. They will spend their money on anything with the name of the person they are collecting in it, even if it's just in a footnote. Like the girl who always comes in asking for Fran Drescher films. And you can't just laugh them out of the store, even though you want to, because they buy the most.

But, you know, these weird people aren't anywhere near as weird as the tape that showed up in a plain manila envelope one day. It had ten American flag stamps on it and no return address. The tape inside was marked in spidery old-lady script. It read "The Chuck Berry Tape."

I put it in the tape deck behind the counter and pressed play. I couldn't stop laughing. That voice. So ridiculously frank. Straining for notes. Trying so hard. Singing old songs, switching over to the voice of a late-night DJ. And the tinkling piano notes between the songs. And the words like bad high school poetry.

Still laughing, I turned it off. I meant to throw the tape right into the trash, but a young girl came in the store looking for advice on Beatles albums. This happens about once a week. So the tape stayed in the deck.

A few days later I had completely forgotten about the manila envelope, but I saw that there was a tape in the deck. I pressed play and that voice came out of the speakers. For some reason—maybe it was me, where I was, what I was thinking, what I was feeling—I heard something in that voice that I hadn't heard before. The more I listened, the more it was there. And I have never since been able to forget what I heard.

⟶

THE CHUCK BERRY TAPE ▶

⟶

That summer, anyone who knew anything had heard of "The Chuck Berry Tape." Jack from the record store made copy after copy, handed them out in coffee shops and while sitting on park benches. Any band in town that was worth anything was listening to it, playing it over and over, tearing the songs and the words and the toy-piano interludes to pieces, and trying to put them back together. New bands were started simply by a couple of people taking a ride with "The Chuck Berry Tape" in the deck of their car radio. They would leave the car shaken, forged together, desperate to create something.

Kay's youngest daughter seemed to have forgotten life outside the room completely. She sat raptly at her lessons, took each persona her mother adopted during the day as factual. Besides mother and teacher, Kay also played the role of school friend, doctor, policeman, and waitress, to name a few. Kay's oldest daughter smiled when she was supposed to, studied when she was supposed to, spoke when she was supposed to, but she felt that her mother and sister were sinking further and further each day. She did not want to follow them.

Some days, flickers of their old life would come through the mess of emptying cans and water bottles and protective talismans. One rainy day, Kay canceled the girls' lessons and they painted one another's face with some Halloween makeup Kay found in a drawer. With her Polaroid camera, Kay took pictures of them all and hung them on the wall. They laughed and hugged and smiled in their simple blue and white and red clown makeup. Kay's oldest daughter almost felt, for a moment, that after the game was over they would walk through the door and back to their normal lives.

They did not. The girls grew skinnier. Kay's youngest had always been thin, but on their diet of canned meat and beans and vegetables, her ribs became grotesquely prevalent. The oldest girl cut her foot on a broken light bulb, and the cut never healed. Kay made light of these developments; the youngest must be auditioning for a job as a swimsuit model, she said, and the oldest's injury was nothing that couldn't be fixed with a Band-Aid. Kay held them close and rocked them, sang them songs. They needn't worry. She was their mother. She would protect them always.

The summer sweltered. The girls each had a birthday. Kay lit candles in their plates of canned food. The oldest looked out the single window in the bedroom, which Kay usually kept locked and shaded, but had opened for the occasion. The green of summer was fading outside into a dull brown that crept over everything. The yard was overgrown and the above-ground swimming pool in the middle of the shaggy trees was greenish black with sludge.

Despite Kay's attempts to keep the room clean, dirt was settling in as if on an abandoned house that lingered, gray, at the edge of town. The mildew in the bathroom spread from the shower to the sink and toilet, black trails of slime in the bowls that came back no matter how many times they were scrubbed away. Spiderwebs hung from corners like lace. Kay and the girls' clothes, which Kay washed in the sink and hung across the backs of chairs to dry, took on a sweet, nauseating odor of rot.

One day when the August heat filled the room with sweat, Kay put down the plans for the lessons she still carried on and announced that the class was taking a field trip to the beach.

The girls dressed in swimsuits and found old floral towels in the closet. It was the first time they had stepped out of the room in months. In single file, Kay led them out the door, down the stairs, and into the overgrown backyard. The burned grass stalks crinkled beneath their feet. Kay marched in the lead like a morbid headmistress. All three of their bodies were as pale as deep-sea fish.

They spread their towels on the deck of the above-ground pool. They relaxed their emaciated, pale bodies onto the towels. There they lay, the dying trees around, the pale wisps of tattered clouds above, the green and black sludge of foul-smelling water below.

When they went back inside, Kay's youngest daughter drew a blue ocean, a yellow sun, and three smiling, happy girls. Kay's oldest daughter drew Auschwitz survivors and crawled into the bathroom to sing. Kay hung the youngest girl's drawing on the wall, kissed her thumb, and made the sign of the cross over it.

In July 1999, *Midi Magazine* interviewed Marshall Black, drummer of the heavy metal band Infamy Into Glory. Black is best known, however, for his work with the experimental rock band Frank. Though Frank released only one album, they were highly influential and are cited as the inspiration to many existing bands, singers, and recording artists. After the release of Frank's single album, their enigmatic lead singer, Jack Tran, disappeared from public view. This interview marks the first time since the release of Frank's single album, *The Chuck Berry Tape Massacre*, that Marshall Black has spoken of Jack Tran, Chuck Berry, and all things Frank.

MIDI MAGAZINE: This new *Infamy into Glory* album, some of it, particularly tracks 5 and 7, sounds a lot like the work you did earlier in your career with bands like Piehole and Wreck. Would you say that this album is a return to your musical roots in a way?

MARSHALL BLACK: I was in Piehole when I was in my early twenties. I've been playing music since I was about thirteen years old. So if you're looking for my roots, they go much further back than that.

MM: So can you give me some sort of idea of your early influences?

MB: Well, shit . . . when I was a kid, I just wanted to play the drums because they were loud. Wanted to bug the neighbors, piss off my parents, you know. But I had this friend Jack who was always playing this weird music for me. Not the stuff you heard on the radio. Most of it didn't make any sense to me at all—I couldn't figure out at the time where he was pulling the stuff out of. Turned out it was pretty standard rebellious-teenager music—the Velvet Underground, Small Faces, Tom Waits. But the moment I first saw drumming as more than hitting tubs when I was pissed off was when Jack played the song "Heroin" for me. You know, every bad music columnist and their mother has taken any chance they can to call the drumming in that song a heartbeat, but, you know, they say it because it's true. It's so true in that way that you can understand only when you're sixteen and alone in your bedroom with your headphones on. Or sitting with the best friend you've ever had, trying to define what music means to the two of you. You know?

MM: I believe I understand what you're talking about.

MB: Yeah.

MM: Can I ask you . . . are you talking about Jack Tran when you say your friend Jack?

MB: The Jack Tran.

MM: You're going to have to excuse me if this is unprofessional, but nobody ever talks about Jack Tran publicly, and I'm just about shitting my pants here.

MB (laughing): You'll have to excuse me, but nobody even knows your magazine exists, so I don't feel like your three loyal readers are exactly the public.

MM: So then feel free to talk.

MB: Where do you want to start?

MM: How about with The Chuck Berry Tape?

⸺⸻⸻⸻⟶

The winter was cold and the cans were running low. All three of them stunk like one big animal that had curled around itself in a winter cave. The water didn't run anymore. The lights didn't go on. Kay sang lullabies and she told stories. Her favorite story was "The Three Little Pigs." She always finished by saying that the third pig's house was made of brick, just like the house they were all in. The safe, safe house where the Big Bad Wolf could never get inside. A kiss and a blessing. Her girls would always be safe.

Kay began to fall apart. She wore her shirts inside out and backward. Her lipstick went over the lines of her lips in broad strokes. Her hair began to gray—or perhaps it had always been gray and there was simply no more dye. Her left eye began to sag down lower than her right, nestled in a soft bag of flesh.

Kay's youngest daughter followed her lesson plans, drew her pictures, and never wondered. Kay's insanity had been her life for too long and she didn't think to question it. Kay's oldest daughter wondered why no one noticed. She was sure that, once, she had been a happy girl in bright dresses who went to her friends' birthday parties. She had sold Girl Scout cookies to neighbors. Didn't these people notice that she was gone? And late at night, when she sang, when those songs reverberated and echoes filled the room and her head, why was she the only one who heard?

———

MB: The Chuck Berry Tape. Well, you know that Jack Tran discovered it, right?

MM: The story is that he found it in the bootleg section of an old record store.

MB: That's partially true. He worked in that record store, and somebody sent it through the mail, no return address. Or so he said.

MM: Why do you add that disclaimer at the end?

MB: Jack Tran was extremely proud to have discovered that tape. And I don't mean to have found it, or heard it first— because on first listen, The Chuck Berry Tape was so bad. I mean cringingly bad. Some little piano being plunked at, that quavery little voice. Jack was proud that he had listened *beyond* that. Jack became obsessed with that tape, more so than any of us that heard it. He swore that underneath the kid's piano, underneath the voice doing imitations and DJ banter that he could hear something real and eternal and human. Some sort of soul in exile and torture.

MM: So why does that make you think there was a return address on the envelope?

MB: I didn't say that. I just said that after the whole story came out, Jack insisted there was no return address. Jack needed there to be no return address. Because otherwise, Jack heard a very human soul in torture and exile, had her home address, and instead of saving her, just made a stupid record album.

———

Kay was dressing up to leave. She had on a high turtleneck from years ago and a fake fur coat. She smelled of mildew and mothballs and a light summertime perfume. She leaned down and kissed first one girl, then the other. In her hand she held a stack of the schoolwork they had done while she conducted lessons. She held her oldest daughter's tapes. She held the pictures with the clown makeup.

"My girls are geniuses," she said to them. The youngest beamed up, listening and believing. "Maybe such geniuses that people will know and want to buy these things to save for when you get older and do wonderful things that no one can ignore. We'll find out. I'll be back soon, and everything will be okay again."

With that, Kay walked through the door.

The girls would never know the reception Kay received in the world outside the room they had been in for so long. The slammed doors, the pity, the charity, the blankness. They never knew because Kay did not come back. Soon, later, or ever.

—⟶

MM: Tell me more about Jack Tran's obsession with The Chuck Berry Tape.

MB: Once he had really heard the tape, his enthusiasm rubbed off on all of us. And I don't just mean the guys in Frank. We made tapes of that tape, passed them out all over the place. By fall there were copies of it in New York and LA and everywhere in between. So it wasn't just Jack. But at the same time, nobody was as obsessed with it as he was. He'd listen to the tape nonstop, front to back and through again. One night he told me that he was sure the girl on the tape was older now, in her twenties. That he thought he was in love with her, and that he would see her one day and recognize her. That she wasn't just on the tape, but also this invisible girl who'd sat next to him on a million late-night drives, that she'd been sitting next to him the first time he heard Elvis Presley. It was a little nuts, but that was Jack. I'd known him since I was a kid. That was the sort of thing I expected from him—to fall in love with some girl he'd never met, who'd made a tape when she was a kid. And, you know, we were just kids. Even then, she wasn't that far away from where we were.

MM: The album you made, *The Chuck Berry Tape Massacre*—what made you call it that? A massacre?

MB: For one thing, Jack put us all through this sort of boot camp of listening to the tape. Nonstop, just like him. In the shower, on our ways to work, *at* work if we could, in our sleep. Then there were the sessions themselves. I mean, they were meticulous, painstaking—but also heavily, intensely emotional. You know track 4 on that album? How the drumming goes from serene to something incredibly intense and maniacal in the space of five minutes?

MM: That's some of my favorite work on the album.

MB: I appreciate that. It felt like evolving from an amoeba in a swamp to a god. All in five minutes. An entire history of evolution, and I experienced every second of it over and over and over until it was perfect. And that was just one song.

MM: Sounds intense.

MB: It was. And that's what Jack demanded from the rest of us every day. After a while, we just started referring to the album as "The Massacre."

———

While her oldest daughter stared at the door, wondering if she should dare walk through it, Kay walked the world outside the room. She walked bewildered under the torrents of wind that whipped clouds back and forth across the sky. She had no idea where she was except under a torn, dark, frightening dome.

MM: The album came out to heavy critical acclaim. It got more college-radio airtime than any other album that came out that year.

MB: Yeah, the album did pretty well.

MM: But after months of critics ranting about Frank being the next important band, after the announcement that a second album would be released in a few months, Frank dropped off the radar. No second album, no nothing. What happened?

MB: It wasn't just what happened to the band, it was national news. Those two girls kept in that room for two years by their crazy mother. You must've seen the pictures of those girls coming out of their house ... It was worse than the naked child running away from Nagasaki. It horrified everyone, the whole country, but nobody as bad as Jack. He just fell to pieces.

MM: How so?

MB: He couldn't do anything anymore, much less play music. I mean, you have to understand—the other boys and I, we put our hearts into that album, everything we could, but don't think for a moment that, start to finish, *The Chuck Berry Tape Massacre* was anybody's baby but Jack Tran's.

MM: But you said earlier—

MB: I don't care what I said. That album belongs to Jack Tran. I've worked with a lot of fine, talented musicians, a lot of extremely capable men and women, but that album I made with Jack is the closest I'll ever come to making something you could call art. It was like being the apprentice who handed Michelangelo brushes while he painted the Sistine Chapel.

MM: And after the girl came out of the room—

MB: He was finished, all that was over. It's hard to explain to someone who doesn't know Jack. This is the guy, remember, who fell in love with this girl from listening to her tape. Who walked down the street thinking one day he'd see her and just know her from that tape. When he saw what had really become of her, he just lost it, you know? He'd always been weird—he used to sleep in the studio holding the original tape while we were recording the album. Holding it like a teddy bear, wrapped around it. But once he saw that little girl walking through the dead grass in her front yard on those spindly legs, blinking and hiding behind her hair . . . He'd show up at our apartments at four a.m., knocking on our doors, crying. You'd take him inside, but all you could get out of him all night was, "Why didn't we help her?" He was always a disaster, drunk or high or just hysterical. Then he came up with this plan that we should all go and find her. She hadn't lived that far away, you know, and Jack wanted us to go there, to look around, to find where she was now and rescue her.

MM: Did anyone agree to this plan?

MB: No one.

MM: Not even you?

MB: No one.

MM: So what happened?

MB: Jack went himself. I don't know how he did it, but he found her. He found the hospital she was in. He got right up to her bedside.

MM: What happened?

MB: All I know is what Jack said. He came into my apartment crying. He couldn't stop. He said she was tied to the bed. She was in some shitty state hospital, tied to a bed. She was screaming and foaming at the mouth. But every now and then, she would stop screaming and sing.

MM: What did he do?

MB: He sat on the floor and cried. He sang with her.

MM: Really?

MB: That's how the story goes.

MM: But is that what really happened?

MB: You'd have to ask Jack Tran that.

MM: But nobody knows where Jack Tran is. He's been as good as nonexistent for the last ten years.

MB: Exactly.

(There is a long pause.)

MB: I think I've said more than I should have. I don't have anything else to say.

It's late at night when the taxi pulls up in front of Marshall Black's house. Marshall's house is light brick and white stucco. It's suburban and nondescript, as if it could disappear and no one would give the empty space it had been in much thought. The man coming out of the taxi looks as if he belongs anywhere but there. He looks as if he knows it, too. His straight black hair falls over his face not for the style but for the anonymity it provides. His features, behind it, are less than a rumor. He steps toward the house hesitantly before stepping back. For a moment he looks as if he will climb back into the taxi and leave.

The taxi waits as he makes his halting way to the door. At any moment, he looks as if he will run back the way he came. When he reaches the door, he does not ring the bell and he does not knock. Still, it is only a moment before the door opens.

Marshall Black pulls the man into an embrace.

"Jack," he says.

Marshall guides Jack into the house. He takes him past the foyer, through the den, down to the basement. In the basement there is a group of about forty people, mostly between the ages of fifteen and twenty-six. They are sitting patiently on the floor. A girl has scars all up her arm. Two boys hold each other's hand. Cigarette burns, jailhouse tattoos. Black eye makeup. Angry eyes. A girl with a bic'd scalp. Inner arms tracked up and ugly. Mouths turned down.

These fearsome children sit patiently on the floor like bad kindergartners who still can't wait for story time. They are waiting for him. Marshall leads Jack to a seat, and there is an acoustic guitar next to that seat.

Jack wants to explain first. There is so much to say. It won't be what they expect, it won't be the same. He heard but he did nothing. He is so sorry.

But they do not want his explanations. In the end, Jack Tran says nothing. He simply plays and sings. And sings.

The Pure

I woke up with a wooden stake held with its point to my heart, as if the lore was true. As if it ever had been.

"What did you do with her?" a voice shouted, shrill and bordering on hysterical. The man's face, which became clearer as I opened my eyes, looked so familiar. He looked so very much like Thane that for a confused moment, I thought Thane had forgotten everything we'd shared and was attacking me for reasons I couldn't yet fathom.

But no. This man was older, his straw-like blond hair graying at the temples. His blue eyes were red-veined and beginning to lack clarity. The shirt that came down to his shaking wrists was conservative, plaid cotton and had white plastic buttons. Thane would look much younger than this for the next few millennia, at least. I woke from my deep daytime sleep, my dreams of old villages and newer crumbling cities, and understood exactly what was happening.

Thane had carried all the sadness in the world when I met him. That was how I knew.

The night we met, I'd been in a pitch-black club shot through with razors of light. My photosensitivity was in full effect; even artificial light in those pulsing, jarring blades can trigger the same unpleasant symptoms I get from the sun. After too much of it, I began to feel sick. Then I began to hallucinate. The blades of white light in the darkness became white-clad angels with flaming swords, the sweat pouring off bodies was suddenly the baptismal water splashed by men in long robes who hid in the shadows. I had to get out and clear my head, so I went to the brick alleyway and lit a joint.

I didn't feel anything from the drug, but it had its desired effect—a person with thin shoulders and so much sadness I could taste it in the air came toward me. Later, I would learn his name—Thane.

Thane couldn't have been more than twenty-five. How much he wished his life was different was palpable. It was in his drunkenness, wobbly and full of desperation. It was in the way he devoured the joint, as if some great prize were at the end. It was in the way he hunched his shoulders to hide the smallest hint of breast tissue still visible beyond the body-damaging ACE bandages wound tight around his chest. I was just another clubgoer to him, a petite woman with long white-blond hair, complexion maybe a bit too pale—but who could tell in the dark club and the alleyway?

I reached out to hand him the joint. The skin of his fingers brushed the skin of mine, electric, wanting.

I didn't want his blood, you know. I never needed his or anyone else's. Humans have always thought their blood so pure and special. Animal blood does fine.

What drew me to him was the sadness I had once known so well.

⟶

We shared a cab back to my apartment. It was a cavern that had once been a warehouse. So few people lived there still, even after most of the rats were chased out and it was divided into units. My blackout curtains, my refrigerator empty but for pouches full of cow's blood—they were too far away from anyone who mattered to matter at all.

"What do you do?" he asked. We were in the car, the driver in front of us glancing up at the GPS map on his phone and pretending to ignore us.

"I manage," I said, shrugging my thin shoulders.

I slid my hand into his. There was something unspoken, as there is in all love. We could not say what we intended. But I did intend the best for him.

Thane stumbled into my apartment as I walked soundlessly in my slipper shoes. Industrial dirt stained the floor. I told him it was best to leave his shoes on if he wasn't in the bed.

"Who are you?" he asked, looking around at the blackness of the floor, the curtains, the sheets on the bed. There was not much in the room. After so long, I have learned that even the things I love don't always come along. I used to leave a place to crowds and fires, to shrill terror and blood. But it's been different. Now it's the whispers that chase me, the rumors of a life lived too long, a face unchanged all those years. When I came here, I came with a suitcase, all my last life's prizes left to gather dust or to be claimed by those brave enough to make their way into abandoned places. Things fade. It is only in the rare moments, the moments that stretch and last and make promises of "forever" they can't keep, that I forget. And, often, it's best to forget what you've left behind. It lets the rest happen.

"I'm just . . . well, I suppose I wonder about you, too?"

"I'm nobody," he said. "Almost gone. Just looking for an okay time."

It was a lie, all of it. He was clinging to life so fiercely. There was fire in him, as small and hot as blue embers you have to kick away the charred wood to reach. "Okay" was the least of what he deserved.

———

I made sure Thane found my supply before anything happened between us. I wanted him to know everything. It's safer that way.

"Are you going to kill me?" he asked, the refrigerator door open and the pouches of cow's blood glowing ruby in its light.

"It's . . . never been that way," I said. "The stories you know—they're from the Pure. Propaganda. Hands with yellow talons reaching for their round-cheeked babies. Carrying their women off. Making their men unholy. Maybe you know stories like that?" I asked.

He closed the refrigerator. "I may have heard one or two of them," he said.

"The only men I've killed have deserved it," I said.

"How? Why?"

"There are men who do bad things," I said. "I wish I could

say just one, but I've lived a number of lives. Anyone would have done the same. I just happen to have the strength to break a neck with my hands."

He paused. "Are you going to turn me?"

I reached my hand behind his head, my fingers tangled in his hair, and kissed him gently, so he would not be afraid.

"The story about having to invite us in?" I asked, leaning my forehead against his. Our eyes could see nothing but each other; our mouths breathed the same air, hot and wet below our line of sight. "That one's almost true."

Thane took his clothes off slowly that night, as if his body was to be a surprise. There are no surprises left, not after a life this long.

Days spent sleeping, nights together. In these moments, I forgot forever was the worst lie.

Thane and I liked to read books together in the warm water that filled the giant claw-footed tub in my bathroom. I am still catching up on what are now called the classics. Imagine the futility of reading all the books of several lifetimes. When humans despair of ever reading the ones released in their own lives, I multiply that by thirty. I will never make it through them all. The edges of my hair brushed the surface of the water, the tips dripping and darkened when I stood to get out.

One gray day, I went to the grocery store. I hadn't been to the one in the city I lived in now, ever, and I found it lacking. I wandered all day to all the vegetable and fish and meat markets within a fifty-mile radius. I picked the ingredients closest to those used in the foods I'd seen favored over multiple lifetimes and many continents. I made brioche, truffled-mushroom soup, game-meat terrine, shucked oysters, miniature beef Wellington with tender cuts of beef. They were all the foods that I had watched others eat with longing after food meant nothing to me. I was so young when I turned that I never experienced the joy I saw on others' faces when they ate them. I cooked these dishes and fed them all to Thane.

I watched him devour them. I understood longing again, in ways I have not for so long.

After many days passed into many weeks, he did not leave the room when I drank from the ruby pouches I kept in my refrigerator. That—it was not longing. It was survival.

———

Once I asked him a question about his childhood, and a smooth blankness fell over his face. He looked up, searched his mind, and found only the slick surface of forgetting. His face contorted; his sharp chin dimpled and went soft.

He couldn't remember. Aftereffects of the electroshock therapy his parents had signed off on when he was younger. It had been designed to make him forget who he was. To be someone else.

Once, he woke up in the day, asking where he was, who he was, who I was. His thin arms and slight back were covered in sweat. He shook. I have seen the fear that was in his eyes only in the hunted.

The light around the edges of the blackout curtains disoriented me, but Thane's fear made me calm. Light could not do to me what had been done to him. I wrapped my arms around him and repeated my name, his name, the date, the street where I lived, the name of the city, the state, the country, the continent, the planet.

⟶

He asked me whether I remembered changing.

"From before," I said, "I mostly remember the sadness."

"What did it feel like?" he said.

"Like being a puppet of yourself, and pulling the strings from just behind. Always apart. I don't know what to say. I remember being my own ghost. Then I was who I am."

He was crying. He cried most nights. We would hold each other's body, our skin pressed close, our mouths together. After, he would weep and shake.

"If I wanted you to, would you change me? Could I stay here? For good?"

I kissed his lips. They were puffy and slick from the tears on his face.

"I *could* only ever do it if you wanted me to. It's never been the way the Pure say it is, all that terror. The Pure's nightmares—for the rest of us, it's just surviving as we are. Impure. Imperfect."

He lay on his back, his arm stretched out to me. "There's so much I've forgotten," he said. "I didn't want it to be gone. I wanted to remember my first bicycle, the color of it, the first time I saw snow—but it's all faded away. When I try to reach it in my head, there's just nothing, like a song lyric or a word you just can't recall. But it's my life."

I touched his face. What was it in this boy that made me want to play games of forever? I knew what a long thing forever was.

"I wish that I could give you those things back," I said, "and make the sadness go."

The door slammed open, spilling sunlight all over. I began to feel nauseated.

"They're threatening to come after me," he said. He was wild with fear.

"Who, Thane? Who?"

"The same doctors, the ones with the electricity. And they'll let them do it again."

"Thane, please calm down."

"No, no," he said. "They can't do it again. You won't let them, will you? You'll change me first? Please, do it now, before they come."

I held him, trying to calm him. "Not now, Thane. Not like this. Not with all this terror."

I closed the door, still feeling sick to my stomach. The darkness wrapped its arms around me, just as I put mine around Thane. He pulled his straw-like hair and wept into his hands. I held him until he fell asleep.

We awoke at sunset. He peeked around the edges of the curtain to the descending orb. It has never been able to hurt me as it is sinking, as the light becomes swollen and orange.

"I still want you to," he said. "I want to stay. I want this forever."

He was calm, collected, so unlike the person he'd been that morning. As he said those words, some of the weight seemed to lift off him.

I rose from the bed. My long hair swept down my back

and I walked toward the window, toward him. In the dying light, I put my mouth on his neck. The taste of his blood ran through my lips, warm, sweet, metallic, him. I had been able to smell the taste of it in his veins since that first night. The longer I kept my mouth on him, the weaker his body went. Not just the life but the sadness was slipping away. I choked on it at first, recognizing its bitterness. But I was stronger than it was. It flowed through me, and away.

Finally, I pulled back. The person he was was gone. There was a long pause before I felt his heart wake up, sluggish at first, then beating with new strength. His limp body, slumped against the wall, stood straight. The ACE bandages had slipped down his flat chest, around his waist. His features had changed, ever so slightly, but I could see how. I could see that all the sadness was gone.

"Hello," he said, blinking, standing in his new self.

"Hello." I smiled.

———

I came fully awake days later, with Thane gone out, and with Thane's father standing over me holding a silly, ineffectual tool of destruction against my chest.

"What did you do to her?" he demanded again. "Where is my daughter?"

He didn't know. He didn't know anything, least of all that I could turn the stake, snap his wrists, destroy him quicker than he could move. And he would deserve it. I didn't doubt that.

He pressed the point against my skin, annoying me but not doing much else.

"She was here," he said. "I don't know what kind of sick thing you've done with her, how you've made her think this is all okay, but I won't have it."

I let him go on for a minute. His daughter. His property. The same old stories of the Pure, with a different name.

Finally, I grew tired. I grabbed the stake and leaped up from bed, so quickly he never saw it coming. In a heartbeat, he was on the floor. I was over him, my eyes wild, my teeth like those he had seen only on beasts, and the point of the wooden stake against his throat.

"You never had a daughter," I hissed at him. "Do you understand me?"

I could see the fear in his eyes. I could smell the fear as his pants went dark and wet with urine. That was one thing Thane remembered from the shock therapy this man had allowed to be performed on him: pissing himself.

"Do. You. Understand. Me?"

"Where is she?" he whimpered.

"You never had a daughter. If you want to keep living, say it with me. Say it until you believe it. I. Never. Had. A. Daughter."

"I . . . never had a daughter."

I made him repeat it until the words became senseless. Only then did I let some of the fire drain from my eyes. I slowly released his collar and pulled the point away from his throat.

"Sometimes it's best just to forget," I whispered to him. The same cruel option he had forced upon Thane. It could be a blessing to forget. Or a torment.

I let him walk out the door, alive, though I didn't trust him not to come back. I could have killed him. Maybe I should have. But I could see the face of the person I loved inside his. For all he had done, Thane would not exist without him. And in a sudden tender space in my heart that I had assumed was long gone, but which had grown in the months Thane and I spent together, I felt that he deserved mercy for that alone.

It didn't matter whether he tried to come back. Tomorrow, Thane and I would be gone. We'd go somewhere else in the world, somewhere beautiful and full of lore. We'd go somewhere where they would never be ready for us, and begin the work of living.

Perseus Denied

"I'm leaving," Belinda said. "I'm getting an apartment across town. Alone."

I looked at her for the first time in a long time. I mean, really looked at her. I'd been busy with my long hours at the hospital, so had she. She'd stopped eating as much, I'd noticed that. I was her husband, how could I not notice the lunches she packed and then brought home uneaten, the dinners she picked around the edges of, the function of her dinner fork magically shrinking into that of a cocktail fork? The woman who stood before me now—her skin was wan and dry, flaky. Her bright blue eyes shone out of her face, the only part of her that seemed to still be alive and vibrant. She was not the girl I had met two years ago. That girl had glowed, radiated life through the pores of her skin.

"But Belinda," I said. I reached for her hand, which she slid away from me, behind her back. She clasped both of her hands there. She looked so sad and sick, her shoulders hunched. "We've been so happy."

"I suppose," she said. I could hear her scratching the dry skin of one arm behind her back. "I ... I can't explain, just now. I've been planning this for a while. I'll be gone by Sunday."

She walked purposefully toward the oak coat hanger near the door. She picked up her heavy winter coat. It seemed heavier than she was, and I had a sudden deep urge to tear it off her thin shoulders, to demand she stay, to tell her I would not allow her to leave. But I didn't. She walked out the door.

By Sunday, all traces of her were gone.

———

We met when she had first moved to town, and I know how that sort of thing never lasts romantically—people latch on when they're lonely, detach when they start to expand their circles—but in about six months we grew together in the way married couples do after decades. We wore the same black plastic-framed glasses. Occasionally we wore each other's shirts. We watched the same movies and had the same thoughts about their meanings, their significance. We read the same books. We both fell in love with Dickens's *A Tale of Two Cities*, sometimes reading chapters of it aloud in bed before we went to sleep. We had similar long-houred jobs, doctors at a local hospital, though in different areas of specialization.

Our first meeting had been at a bar where doctors and residents often went after long shifts. She was eating french fries, a huge plate of them, what looked like a double or triple order. She did not share. She did not pause to talk, even though others we knew from the hospital were there. She just kept eating and eating, occasionally taking a huge swig of beer. I wasn't sure where she was fitting all that food in her tiny frame. Her small, fair body seemed to be taking in more calories than it could possibly use in a year. I was a little disgusted, but also strangely entranced. I watched her eat from the corner of the bar until there wasn't a single french fry left on the plate. When she was finished she stood up and came over to me, said she knew me from the hospital, asked what I was drinking, made small talk. I offered her a sip of my coffee-caramel craft beer and she took it, drinking a quarter of the pint.

We slept in the same bed that night, and many nights after. I didn't have time to go out and socialize much, and meeting her seemed perfect. She was exactly what I wanted, and she had almost fallen into my lap. Within a few months, we were inseparable.

After a year marriage had seemed like the best choice, and we eloped. We didn't have time for wedding planning, or the hassle and potential disappointments from family and friends. We just went to the courthouse on a day we both had off. By then, the tiny blonde girl I had married had a big round belly. She wasn't pregnant. She was just happy, eating, growing. I loved her all the same, but sometimes I gently suggested she exercise. For her health. I said it more than once, I suppose, but it seemed as if she never heard. I came up with a diet for her at one point, a healthy one full of fruits and vegetables, balanced and nutritious. She had looked at the paper I'd written it on, looked at me, looked at the paper.

Maybe this was why, I thought when she left.

She packed everything and left while I was at work. When I came home, there was just an absence where she had once been. Her side of the closet was empty. She'd washed the bedclothes before she'd gone, as if to make sure I wouldn't be startled by a stray blond hair in a week's time. Her side of the bed would never be wrinkled again, her pillow would never smell like her shampoo. Her pictures were gone, her books holes on the shelf. All I could feel was the nothingness of a story's abrupt, unsatisfying end.

She stopped coming to work, just like that. When I went to our HR department (we were still married, she was still legally my wife), they told me she'd put in notice weeks ago, removed her direct deposit that went into our shared account, and said she'd be back for her final check. In other words, there was no address for them to forward anything to. The woman from HR looked at me kindly. My hands were shaking.

———⟩

She's still mine, I kept telling myself. *She'll come back. She has to.*

She did not come back.

Three weeks after she left, I decided to find her.

I searched in every way I could. After work, I would ride the bus late at night, into the parts of town I did not know, into the red bricks and cobblestone streets. I rode under the graffitied train trestles, past the burst of activity at midtown, through the abandoned factories, across bridges, and to the dim and winding streets far on the other side. Cars became fewer as the nights became later, the city almost abandoned. I would walk into alleys and haunt the outsides of the kinds of bars I'd never imagine her at in our old life. In this new life, in this new part of the city, anything felt possible. The city seemed strange and foreign, as if she and I were engaging in some sort of sweeping chase around the world. That seemed a little romantic to me.

Things started to fall apart a bit at work. I wasn't sleeping. A patient walked into the ER, and I misdiagnosed her with a case of the flu and sent her home—she came back later vomiting blood. I'd missed the easy-to-spot signs of a hemorrhaging ulcer. I vowed to sleep more after that, but when nighttime came, I still searched.

One day, a man walked into the ER. He looked absolutely fine, and when the nurse checked his vitals, they were fine, too. I took my time getting to him, with all the chaos of a usual night in the city happening—the stabbings, the shootings, the homeless people half frozen to death who'd been peeled off the streets. When I finally pulled aside the curtain that was separating him from the people on either side of him, he looked up from the bed in a way that felt dismissive. Maybe it was how *I* was looking at *him*. He was young, in his early twenties, the sort of rock-and-roll demeanor that I usually associated with little work ethic and a fairly low social value. He wore tight black jeans, motorcycle boots, and a printed T-shirt that clung to his thin torso. He looked absolutely healthy.

"What's the problem tonight?" I asked.

"I mean, not a problem, like, a worry more, I guess."

"You're in the ER for a worry?"

He shrugged his thin shoulders. "No health insurance. You have to look at me, legally."

I sighed inwardly. "Okay. What can I help you with?"

"Look, this is going to sound weird."

"I bet I've heard weirder in the middle of an ER," I reassured him. But my voice was a little tight, I suppose.

"I think I might've caught some weird kind of STD," he said.

"That doesn't sound weird at all." It could've been taken a few ways.

"Here's the thing," he said. His verbal tics were beginning to annoy me. "I met this girl, she just moved into my building. Pretty. Blonde. Kinda weird skin thing going on, but, you know. Great body and all, so . . ."

I froze as he paused. Belinda?

"So we have a few drinks, one thing leads to the next, and the next thing you know I'm in her bed. But she's not fucking me. She's rubbing her skin all over me."

I took a deep breath. My hands were shaking. I grabbed his wrist, maybe a little too hard, definitely a little too hard, and looked at his arm.

"You look fine," I said, loosening my grip. "You can't get STIs that way. Scabies, staph infection, ringworm—none of which you have—but not STIs. Go home. Wear condoms. Google safe sex practices. Be angry public education failed to provide you with them. Pick your sexual partners a little more carefully."

He looked relieved.

After he left, I looked at his chart. I took a quick picture of his address with my phone.

Later that night, standing outside the address, looking at the ground-floor window of a tall brick building, I saw Belinda in the yellow light of a lamp.

That first time I stood there, the city din crackling all around me, I began to wonder who I was.

It wasn't the last time I'd stand there. I went once a week after work at first, careful to take the bus after hers, careful to walk at least a block behind. She looked sick. Her skin was flaking off in psoriasis-like chunks, and she was losing weight by the day. Maybe, I told myself, she was dying. Maybe she had some incurable disease that she had wanted to spare me the grief of. Maybe she had the extremely rare peeling skin syndrome, but a deadlier variety than had been seen before. I was sure she still loved me; people's lives couldn't intertwine like ours and then just fall apart. I hadn't had great role models for love. My grandparents and my parents were divorced, all of them hated each other. But somewhere I had gotten it into my head that marriage was forever. The only logical reason that she could be leaving me was to spare me some sort of pain.

I watched her in her new place, alone. There was no furniture that I could see. Here and there, in little piles on the floor, were her books and clothes. I thought back to when we met, when she moved into my apartment. She'd had even less then. She'd been new to the city.

Night after night, I'd go there, hide myself down the alley. I'd watch her scratch at her dry skin, watch her drag herself from one end of the tiny apartment to the other, her energy obviously low. My wife was dying. She had to be.

One day, when I arrived after my shift at the hospital, she wasn't there. Her light was on. But she did not appear in it. She did not walk back and forth. Her books and clothes remained untouched. She was just gone. The emptiness rang out of her window.

After three days without seeing her, I waited for a building resident to walk inside and called for her to hold the door. She obliged, and we chatted a bit about the building, me making things up and pretending to agree with things she said, before she walked up the stairs to her apartment. I walked to where I knew Belinda's apartment was.

The door was open. The light that looked warm and yellow from outside was a harsh, bare bulb hanging from the ceiling. The room was empty. The whole place was empty. Except the bed.

In the bed, there was a large dry husk of skin. Not bloody. It was not a murder scene, or a death scene. There was a fragile shell in the shape of my wife.

———

I kept working. I worked until I collapsed in bed every night. I took extra shifts. I didn't look for her. She was gone.

I waited for a death certificate, but one never showed up. After the appropriate amount of time, I filed for a divorce in absentia. Against all reason, I harbored a brief, bright hope that she would show up in court when the day came. She did not.

Years later, I met a girl, a resident at the hospital I had become a chief physician at. She was bright and driven and cultured. I didn't fall in love with her right away, but I knew I shouldn't let her go. We eventually married.

We had been out to a play one night and were walking

home in the dark. We were arguing, as we sometimes did, about the meaning of what we had just seen. We often disagreed. It felt healthy. Sometimes we liked to prove each other wrong.

I looked away from my second wife and down the street to the theater. I could see in the distance, coming closer, a couple. A man and a woman. As they came closer and closer, I was struck by how alike they looked. Same dark, short hair. Same striped shirts, though worn differently. There was something about the woman, though. Something so familiar. It was the shine of her skin, radiating out of her pores.

"Be-belinda?" I said suddenly as they passed. I hardly ever thought the name anymore, and it felt as if it had come from somewhere hidden. The woman turned and looked at me sharply.

"I'm sorry, I think you have the wrong person," she said.

"Weird," she and her partner said in unison, as they walked away.

I turned back to my second wife. The fight had gone out of me.

"Who's Belinda?" she asked.

I made a short reply about an old friend. I did not say anything to her about my first marriage, ever, other than that it had existed.

I Was There, Too

Broom into the corners, mop into the corners. Over and over, my job. I've made some bad decisions, I know. I guess not as bad as the ones the guys who end up in the hole made.

Matthew Miner. I first saw him when I went to clean out his cell. I'd heard about him, yeah. That guy. The one who killed all those people. Put here, in the hole, for his own protection. From the guys like he'd been, outside, before the killings, and from the guys he'd hated outside. Nobody wanted a guy like him around.

I thought about my girlfriend, outside this pit, every time I thought about quitting. Every time I ended up mopping up shit, or puke, or even, that one time, skin. She was pregnant. She was having our baby, which we'd decided to keep, even though. So I slid my mop over concrete floors and whatever was on them, and I thought, Life could be worse. It's been worse.

And then Matthew Miner came along.

He didn't look like the monster you'd imagine. No swastika tattoos on his face. No glowing red eyes. Those were the kinds of things in my head when I heard about him, first, when my boss told me I'd have to go mop down the floors in solitary where they were keeping him.

"Real sicko," he sighed. "When they took him to jail he was covered in brains and blood. Eyes nowhere. Looking like he didn't have a soul."

That part bothered me, maybe most. No soul. It was one of those things. I still believed, a little, in the stuff I learned as a kid. Souls in bodies, keeping them human. Things you could trade away for drugs or women or a guitar at the crossroads, and die empty. Things you could hang on to, if you tried real hard, after your whole shit life. And those moving through the world without, filled with evil instead. Evil, I've seen it. I've seen men who can kill another man. Nothing there. Just like the boss man said. Eyes nowhere.

So I guess I expected that, when I went into the hole to mop. I took a deep breath, when the boss man opened the door with his keys, and thought of that little tiny something in my girlfriend's stomach. I thought of it growing into a boy or girl with dark hair and eyes and skin somewhere between my and my girlfriend's tones. Running around. Laughing like a crazy person at some new toy, or the new puppy I'd buy one day. Took that breath. Walked in.

Matthew Miner didn't say a word to me that first time. Just watched me. Quiet. Damn near jumped from my skin when he coughed.

Broom into the corners, mop into the corners. In and out. I took a long shower when I went home that night, like his breath on me could turn me into him.

⟶

Sometimes, a lot of times, the worst things go through my head. I try not to tell them to my girlfriend. But I think about this baby, about the guys like Miner. I think about the world we're putting this beautiful little baby into. And if it's a boy, I think about him getting shot, just about every day. I can picture it so clear, the bullet wrecking his little-kid face. He's never more than thirteen in my head when it happens. And life going on, without him. Yeah, I don't tell my girlfriend.

And if it's a girl, I picture some sick shit. All these guys, guys like I used to be once, not even guys like Miner. Saying the wrong things to her. Doing worse. And then I think about the guys like Miner. And I think for the millionth time, Not into this world. Not now. Not our baby.

But the baby's coming. We put away as much as we can of my paychecks, and try to save up our food stamps. And I can't quit. I can't walk out, like I've done over and over in the past. And when Miner started talking to me, that was when I wanted to leave the most.

Putting the broom into the corners, and before I got to the mop, he said, "It's real hard, once you see the truth."

And I froze. Broom stopped. Couldn't even pretend it was okay.

I turned toward him. The room was dark, the lightbulb a low wattage. He was sitting on the single bed, in the corner. It was damp in there, not like the walls were leaking but still damp. Maybe a leaky pipe on the toilet on the side of the room I was sweeping. Told myself that was why I shivered all the way down my spine.

I opened my mouth, but he went on.

"People don't know," he said. "They don't know. They think you're some fringe weirdo, some keyboard warrior—they don't know you're trying to help them. It's like the emperor's new clothes, you know? The guy's naked? And nobody wants to say? That's how it is when you're one of the ones who see the truth."

I tried to see his eyes, there on the bed. Looked hard. Didn't see much in the dimness. I started mopping. He sat there, staring. Mop into the corners. Me out of the room as fast as I could.

Couldn't sleep that night. I lay there in bed, my girlfriend's skin warm under the blankets, me not wanting to touch her with my cold hands. Like all of me was made of ice. Kept thinking about that man sitting on that bed, about the thing he thinks is the truth. That truth would have my baby dead before it's born. I rubbed my hands together until they were a little warmer. I kept rubbing them, trying to start a fire, almost, under the blankets. When they were finally warm, I reached over and put one on my girlfriend's stomach. Stupid. I couldn't feel that baby, it was too soon. My girlfriend, sleeping, winced away from the still-cold of my hands and rolled over.

Rolled back on my back, then, thinking. The way you see the world. Your truth. How can we look at the same input, get different worlds? Big thoughts like that, I don't care for them. I started thinking about life as computer simulations, like in that old movie. It'd make sense, how far off some people get in their truth, if we were all walking around seeing just what we saw, some sort of bubble. But no. I can't think that steep, even when my mind strolls around at night, when I should be sleeping. All the input we get, where does it come from? How does the world make the baby growing and squirming in my girlfriend, and the man in that cell? I thought these thoughts until I couldn't anymore, and fell asleep.

The hole got mopped but not by me, not for a few days, a week. I couldn't stop thinking about Matthew Miner though. I spent a lot of time, most lunch breaks, reading articles about him on my junk phone. Not an iPhone, not by a lot. I'd known, before then, a lot of the words that followed Miner. White supremacist. Neo-Nazi. Alt-right. I'd even heard about Pale Man, some excuse he'd babbled, covered in the brains of his friends. But it wasn't until I started looking that I found out who Pale Man was. And that's when sleep got up and left the building for a while.

First I saw the memes that Miner had made. The original ones, ones he posted up on some website that looks pretty whackadoodle, if you know what I mean. I looked at its wonky script and early-internet style on my phone, and wondered how people spent their lives there. And those people, those lives. Man. I've made some mistakes. But not mistakes like these guys'.

Those early memes were from a contest. The rules weren't explicit in what these people were about, but they were the judges, so all the entries were a little off-kilter, *way* off-kilter, hateful, cruel. Miner's memes had been the most hateful of all, I guess. So they won. I pictured his hands moving over a keyboard, making these images, while my hands detail-cleaned a room, the crevices, the edges. In his mom's basement, that's where he'd made this stuff.

The first one, the one that won the contest, was one of the old integration photos. You know, the ones with white people on one side, screaming as Black kids got let into schools, or used water fountains, or sat at lunch counters.

But they weren't historical, not after he got done. This figure was added into them. A tallish guy, dressed in a black button-down and slacks. His hair was white-blond, cut close on the sides and a little longer on top. That new neo-Nazi style, the respectable skinhead look. The figure's skin was so white that it obscured most of his features. Except his smile. It was more blinding white framed by a darker outline of lips. With everybody in the picture so emotional, he looked really out of place just standing there, smiling. Underneath the picture, in big white block letters, Miner had placed the words: I WAS THERE, TOO.

That got me for a while. This guy. Skin whiter than mine, smile as full of terror as a shark's. I wondered what kind of head you'd have to have to make him, to put him there. The other posts had come in rapid succession after that one won the contest. There was a picture from South Africa of Black people lining up to get their papers to work in the white areas. The blinding-white-skinned, shark-smiled man was in one of them, too, his face out of place. He didn't belong, even though the photo alteration was seamless. Underneath it, Miner had put the words: I WAS THERE, TOO.

There were a few more photos from big moments. You know. Gruesome times. The camps where they'd offed the Jews, a march where the police were cracking skulls. That man, that pale ghost of a man had been stuck in all of them. And the words: I WAS THERE, TOO. It created a picture across time. Something Miner, it seemed, had been proud of. History. Heritage. Whatever words these guys put on hate.

There was something I couldn't understand, though. The turn. Matthew Miner had been arrested after the next-door neighbors of a basement apartment called the police, when they heard rapid fire, extended bursts of gunshots. Found covered in the brains and balls and blood of a gathering of neo-Nazis. Blubbering through the blood on his lips, over and over, the words, "Pale Man."

Next time wasn't as hard. Mop, broom, all that, but I went in wishing he'd talk to me. Wishing he'd tell me. Knowing maybe he'd look at me and see someone he could talk to. Someone he thought might be like him.

I had questions. I didn't ask any, not right away. Mop in the bucket, sloshing the water. It's what I do. With my high school education, my life of mistakes, it's the best I've done, the steadiest. That baby's coming. So I mop.

I was mopping up the excess water when he looked at me. Those eyes. Couldn't see them in the dark, except as darkness. Shadows set in his face.

I cleared my throat. "Let me ask you something," I said. I tried to sound like people expect me to. Me with my shitty tattoos on my neck and hands. Me with my mop and broom.

"You?" he asked. "Want to ask me?"

"That Pale Man," I said. "How the hell did you come up with something like that?"

He smiled. A little. A shadow deepened on one side of this face, that's it.

"I'm good with photoshop," he said. "Really good. I spend a lot of time on memes. They're a kind of art—but not that bullshit kind that you have to go to some stupid school for."

Memes, he said. Pictures and words. The hobby of a guy who could blow away a meeting full of his best friends.

"But that's not the story you want to hear," he said. He leaned forward, his face coming a bit into the light of the bare bulb hanging down. "The story you want to hear is how Pale Man took over."

Chills up my back, up the backs of my arms. He knew. Of course he knew. I didn't care about some meme contest on the internet. Made sense, that part. Neo-Nazi comes up with white supremacist symbol, spreads it around the hate sites. I spend longer on those sites than I care to. Reading about how the Holocaust never happened. Reading about the struggle of the white man. Reading about men's rights. About how the history books lied, how there was a global Jew conspiracy.

"Once I made him," Miner was going on, "he was out of my hands. Spread like wildfire. Had a backstory that went all over the world, had videos about him, spread through the history of everything. There he was. My creation." Miner looked me up and down. "A guy like you know anything about what I was getting at? The truth I was getting to with Pale Man?"

I stood there leaning on my mop. I said no, the talking stopped. I said yes, I was a lie. I couldn't bring myself to lie about that hate. So I said nothing.

"The truth is a funny thing," Miner said, nodding once. "You'll see."

⟶

You'll see.

I went out for a drink that night. Just one. Then two. I hadn't been out drinking in weeks, not since the lines had appeared on the pregnancy test. Two lines, crossed. My whole life changed. I thought about it. I thought about what *the truth* was for Matthew Miner. I kept thinking. I drank another beer. Stumbled into my apartment at three a.m. to screams and my girlfriend throwing soft things that could never hurt me in my direction. Stuffed animals we'd bought for the baby's room, packs of tissues. It was almost a joke, but she was so mad. I was out of breath. Thought someone had been behind me for a while on the street walking home. Didn't say anything, I didn't want to scare her. Tried to grab her wrists, but she kept twisting away. Didn't want to hurt her, so I just took it.

My head was pounding the next morning, and the thought of that piss-smelling mop made me want to vomit. I called off work while she stood over me with her coffee.

"You said the drinking was over," she said.

"I'm sorry," I said. My head was splitting. She didn't know a thing about Matthew Miner, other than what we all knew from the news. Not that I'd seen him. Not that he'd been talking to me. I wasn't going to tell her, ever.

———

Pale Man got out of Miner's hands quick. All over the internet, like a disease. I don't use the internet much. Sometimes I repost pictures I see on Facebook. But I'd never seen Pale Man until I got to looking.

There were sites dedicated to the timeline of Pale Man. That was where I learned about the turn the meme had taken.

"When Pale Man Got Claimed by the SJWs," a section headline on one of them read. It had an earlier meme that Miner had done, one of the originals. But instead of saying, "I WAS THERE, TOO" underneath it, it read on top, "this white-lead chapter about whiteness," and on the bottom, "is but a white flag hung out from a craven soul." What the hell did that even mean? Site went on to say that this was when the internet had decided that Pale Man wasn't the pride symbol that Miner had intended. Pale Man was some creature lurking on the edges of humanity. A boogeyman. Eyes with no soul behind them. Pale Man, now, was some demonic force that made the rightness in humanity go wrong.

That's what I'd seen in Pale Man from the first image. I guess others had, too. Miner and those guys, they were outnumbered by the ones who thought like us. That made me feel okay for a moment. Like the baby in my girlfriend was going to be okay in this world. But then I thought about it more. Pale Man—even as a demon—was still out there.

"He gets in your head," one story that had popped up around that time said. "He lurks at the edges. One day you see him. And you can't unsee him, not ever again. And then he's all you can see. Until you do the worst thing you can imagine."

And that could happen to anybody. Even Matthew Miner, stumbling into custody with those white supremacists' brains all over his face.

            ⟶

I didn't stay out late, ever. When it got dark, I always thought someone was following me down the street, steady and slow.

I started having these thoughts, sometimes. They weren't mine. They weren't the things that had been in my head, ever. They were like someone else's voice whispering in my ear. These whispers, these thoughts. Terrible things. I'd lie in bed at night with my girlfriend, that baby growing in her, and my mind flashed with all the worst things humanity could do.

———

I would go online to look things up. Something I'd never really done in the past, but there was so much out there. I'd start somewhere like "first trimester of pregnancy" and end up at Pale Man. Always that face, that pale face, those shark teeth. I'd start at "common birth defects" and I'd end up at Pale Man. I'd start at "interracial families" and I'd click one link, then another, then another, and before I knew it I'd gotten to Pale Man. It felt like he was at the end of everything. Waiting.

Meanwhile, Miner got chattier. Liked the guy with the broom. Thought he could trust me. Maybe it was the tattoos on my neck, my hands, even though there was no swastika or anything marking me like him. The guys that like me in the hole, in the prison, they always seem to like my tattoos. He got to telling me about his "cunt mother" who turned him in, about how much he hated Jews. How guys like us had to stick together. I nodded, but I didn't say anything. He said enough.

One day, without asking, he was telling me about the murder. It was no secret, he'd confessed. There would be trial and all that, but he'd told the cops already what he told me that day. I just pushed the broom while he talked. Real slow and even.

"That day, I told some of the guys I had something important to tell them. That's the last thing I remember. The rest is images, but I'm not there—I'm watching through the window or from outside the door, or somewhere.

"I walk in like always, the places where we talk the real talk, make the real plans. I see it from outside. That stuff on the internet, yeah, we spend a lot of time on it. But the real things—they happen in these basements, in these sheds out back, in places where we leave our phones outside and get away from our computers and our Alexas. I walk in like always, but when Ray hugs me, I pull out my Ruger and put it to his head and then his head is gone and then the others are reaching for their guns, all my friends, all the guys who I've been drinking and planning and beating people with, and their fingers fumble because they're so surprised, but mine don't because the Pale Man is guiding me, making me do the worst thing I can think of, take out the people who belong, who are the ones I should be protecting with my life, who I have protected, who I *want* to protect. First I shoot Rich in the stomach and his blood pumps, like a hole in a swimming pool. Then I shoot Marty in the arm, right below his swastika tattoo, because I miss where I aimed, and he grabs the bullet hole and looks at me and looks down at the gun he dropped and starts to cry because of the distance between him and the only thing that can save him. And I shoot him in the forehead. And James, he gets one in the balls, then the legs, because he's last, and why not play a little, after he's defenseless? When I finally shoot him in the face, he's squirting blood from everywhere, and the person inside me is laughing while outside I'm wondering why I would ever kill these people. And before long I'm back in my body, and my body is covered in their brains and I'm just standing there smiling."

He didn't move or flinch when he said any of it. Related it like the weather. The day Pale Man came for him, made him do the worst thing he could think of. Something that maybe wasn't so bad for the rest of us, but that's not what Pale Man does. He gets in your head, you see, and it's the worst *you* can think of. Maybe you're a neo-Nazi like Matthew fucking Miner, sitting there on your bed in the hole, now suddenly cry-laughing because Pale Man is real, real, real, something you made up is out there in the world. Or maybe you're a guy like me who lies in bed at night, thinking words like *abomination* when you think of the sweet baby growing inside your girlfriend's brown belly, a word you never thought, but you try it on, and there it is, and then there is the thought of the butcher knife in the kitchen and the thought of all that blood, pumping in their bodies, her growing one and the baby's still tiny one. Maybe it's driving you crazy, keeping you up at night, maybe the sound of that broom on the ground in the hole where you stand as you hear the story of Matthew Miner's murders is enough to set you over the edge, to make you want to scream, a story and a scream like a howl. Maybe you throw the broom down and run out, you don't give a fuck about this job, you can't take one more minute of standing there with that man—the real abomination—and you run out, past your boss with his mouth open like a caught fish, and you run past the time clock and you run home and you put your face on your girlfriend's stomach, who is crying, but no one followed you home, no one followed you, you are safe, you are in yourself, not standing outside, there are no shark teeth whispering in your ear, and there are bad things in the world, but they are not here, not inside you, not yet, not the way they could be, and you promise her you will find something else quick, that you will take care of both of them and that you will never let the monster in.

Hinkypunk

The summer that Susan was eighteen, the stretched, sweaty, distant summer on the marsh, the summer that she pulled me aside to tell me that love knew things that Grandmother and Mother and Father did not, the summer that Susan retreated and collapsed—that was the summer of the hinkypunk.

I didn't have the words for it, the first time we saw it. It was a taste in my mouth, the hollow bitterness that settled into the back of my throat after Grandmother let me sip her coffee in the morning, but also somehow the oil-slick feel of butter on corn from the garden that stretched down one side of the property. It was a burst, and then the residue on the air, the smell, the soot.

Grandmother, Jack, and I sat on the porch that jutted off the back of her house and high above the marsh. We sipped sweet tea out of the long, cold glasses that Grandmother always served it in. Grandmother and I swung gently on the bench swing that hung from the roof of the porch, and Jack sat near us, all long, gangly legs and jutting elbows, on what looked like a stool hewn by hand from a large tree trunk. His body twisted around, awkward and newly teenaged, as he scratched at the mosquito bites that dappled his legs. Inside the house, in our bedrooms, the laundry had piled up for five days. Though I couldn't hear her, I knew that Susan was inside, her eyes open in the dark, weeping.

"What was it?" I whispered. The burst of yellow and orange and blue and white had flashed into the darkness, then out of it, like a birthday candle in front of an eager child.

"Ignis fatuus," Grandmother said, after holding a sip of the sweet, brown liquid in her mouth as if she was chewing it, then swallowing. "Will-o'-the-wisp. Hinkypunk."

I traced the last word—hinkypunk—in the cursive I was learning on the arm of the bench swing.

"But what *is* it?" I asked again.

"Gases from the marsh," Grandmother said. "Lit up like spirits. But really: nothing. Nothing."

She smoothed the tangles of my hair as I had seen her do to Susan earlier, while Susan lay in bed unmoving. Then Grandmother had whispered, "It's for the best. You don't see it now, but it's for the best."

The morning after the hinkypunk, the Sheriff came. Grandmother didn't know how to wash her own clothes, to clean her own home. She hadn't yet begun to look for someone to replace Lorna, who had replaced the woman who came before her, who had replaced the woman who came before her, a steady string all the way back to Grandmother's childhood in the acres around the marsh.

Grandmother opened the door a crack, still in her nightgown, and begged a moment to pull herself together. We were unaccustomed to her lack of composure, and when she hissed at us to clean the kitchen table and sink *quickly*, we did. In less than fifteen minutes, she was perched on the seat at the head of the table, clothes perfect, makeup applied, coffee brewing. She commanded Jack to let the Sheriff in. He followed her directions laconically, his face hard at the morning interruption.

I sat on the couch primly, as Grandmother had instructed in a hissed whisper I knew not to disobey. I arranged my skirt around me on the couch cushion while Jack slunk around the corner and back to his room. Lucky, I remember thinking, that he could avoid what I couldn't then put quite into words—the pretending to care what adults said while simultaneously minding one's own business, which my age required. He was thirteen then, old enough to get away.

The Sheriff and my grandmother chatted amicably as she poured them both coffee. These were the grandchildren, then, Lanie's? he asked. He had heard about the ongoing divorce; would Lanie be back down to get them at the end of the summer, would she stay? Hearing my mother Elaine's nickname from this stranger's mouth shocked me into the awareness that she had once lived a life full of people whom I had never laid eyes on. The narcissism of my childhood had been struck one blow that summer, when Mother and Father sent the three of us away while they finalized their divorce, and had thus been softened for the one it suffered in that moment. Still, the Sheriff—this solid, broad-shouldered, tan-uniformed man—called her the name that Grandmother called her only occasionally, in moments of warmth. Had he once, maybe when she was Susan's age, held my mother's hand? Kissed her? The thoughts piled on top of one another, crowding my head.

Finally, Grandmother put down her coffee cup with a distinct noise that signaled the end of their small talk and my idle thoughts.

"Why are you here, George?"

He breathed out. It wasn't a sigh, not quite. But even I could hear the regret in his words.

"The girl," he said. "Things aren't like they used to be."

Grandmother did not speak for a moment. She stirred her coffee with the spoon she'd laid down next to it. It didn't need stirring. When she looked up, her wet blue eyes were a storm.

"Don't I know it, George."

"She's gone," the Sheriff went on. "No trace. Her mother at the courthouse, the police station, making a stink you can smell a mile away. Last place she was seen was here, working."

"George, let me ask you—am I supposed to know where and how every time some child runs off?"

"Grown woman, ma'am," he said. "Twenty-two years old."

"Mentality of a child," Grandmother insisted. "Left work midday and never came back, even to finish her cleaning. The place has been a disaster, and you know how hard it is finding someone these days, since all Johnson's nonsense and all this empowerment."

"That may well be," the Sheriff said. "It sounds *likely*. Girl probably ran off north or west, wanting to be a star or join some movement. But that mother. At the station every day, ma'am. Things aren't like they used to be."

The silver ricochet of Grandmother's spoon off the insides of the coffee mug filled the room. I looked toward the window, then back.

"The mother says she saw Lanie's oldest with her, ma'am," the Sheriff said, looking down. "More than once."

Grandmother's lips sucked in and her chin jutted out. "Nonsense."

"It's just what she says, ma'am," the Sheriff looked back up under his eyelashes. "Can't always put stock in that. I asked her, you know, what they'd be doing together. She couldn't give me a satisfactory answer to that." He paused. "Where is the oldest now?"

"I think you'd better go," Grandmother said.

"Of course, ma'am. We both have other things that need to be done," he said, standing. He picked his hat up off the table, asking Grandmother to give Lanie his best.

———

We'd been raised in a suburb of Boston, far away from my mother's southern roots, far away from the nickname Lanie and the easy drawl and the wet heat of my grandmother's house. That summer was a shock for all of us, but most of all for Susan. My beautiful, tall, long-limbed sister, Susan. Her wheat-blond hair thicker and lighter than either Jack's or mine, just like my father's, where we'd been given our mother's limp mouse-brown locks. Susan who couldn't be told anything she didn't want to hear. Susan who was eighteen and so beautiful that I'd never known anyone who didn't fall in love with her at least a little. Susan who spoke what she meant as if the world waited to hear it.

She'd just finished high school. She was ready for a break, a summer with her friends, some time to decide on what came next in life. She had argued with our mother and father about joining the Peace Corps and going off to college. The compromise reached had been that she would wait a year and think about both, and if she met the man she would marry in that time, then everything was decided anyway. She wouldn't back down, and I knew that soon she'd be living out the life of one of Kennedy's young world ambassadors or studying law. But instead of having a summer to think and spend time with friends, Susan was shipped off to our grandmother's house, along with the rest of us, as our parents decided things for themselves. Instead, there were the clandestine hands that slipped into each other the moment they suspected no one was looking. There was the electricity I could feel, even so young, so far removed from its sources. Susan fell in love: not with the right man, whom my parents hoped she would marry and raise children with, but with Lorna, the woman who cleaned our grandmother's house.

———————

The night that the Sheriff came to the house, we saw the hinkypunk again. Years later, I would see a fire blower in a circus, and in that moment, in that tent, crushed between the shoulders of the other audience members, I would feel a chill down my spine, uncontrollable and fierce. I would remember all the nights on that high porch above the marsh. I would remember the single spire of flame that lifted up into the sky, then snapped out of existence. The grabbing of air in a *woosh*, the eating of it, and its combustion in front of me. The warm, mossy smells of the marsh. My brother Jack's legs dangling over the ledge of the porch, the fire reflected in his dark eyes.

"Grandmother?" I said.

"I *told* you," she said. "Happens from time to time. Marsh gases."

"Why can't you just *listen?*" Jack said. As he'd grown in the last year, so had any remaining sweetness from his boyhood been drained away. He was turning into a man, a strange, alien creature, from the boy I had grown up with. All his words were harsh these days, when he spoke at all. Even orders from our grandmother were met with a sullen look— not so sullen she could be tempted to snap at or slap him, but sullen enough that I always saw.

"But why . . ." I asked. Jack picked up an errant stick that had fallen from a tree and onto the porch. He poked it between the wooden slats of the porch. My voice fell down to a whisper, ". . . why did they appear just when Lorna disappeared?"

The silence was astounding, broken only by the dry sounds of bark peeling back as Jack's motions became quicker and more violent. After several minutes of it, Grandmother stood and walked toward the door.

"If you wish to believe superstition rather than fact," she said, as she disappeared into the darkness inside, "then you may sit here and be afraid."

Grandmother's house at night was a symphony of creaks and cracks, noises she said were "the old house settling." If you stepped on a floorboard, its report bounced off the walls; if you inched open a door, it sang its crescent path out for the whole night to hear.

Stepping carefully out of the bathroom one night that summer, I inched around the loudest floorboard and found the cavern of Susan's open bedroom door. She slept in the room that had once been our mother's. Jack slept in the room our uncle had once slept in, and I had been given the room with the least steady history—the guest room.

As I stepped from the hallways into the blackness of Susan's room, my eyes adjusted. The room felt hot and wet, a combination of the growing thunderstorm and the tears that I could sense Susan was crying in the darkness.

My eyes adjusted to the weak starlight coming in through the window. Susan, my beautiful sister, lay in the bed with her honey-blond hair a mess of unwashed tangles. She lay flat on her back, and tears rolled, unstoppable, from the corners of her eyes, down the sides of her face, into the seashell curve of her ears, down her neck. She must not have seen or heard me come in. When I slipped my hand into hers on the mattress, something like hope flickered across the black pool of her eyes in the dark.

"It's me, Suze, it's me," I whispered. Just like that, the life went back out of her.

"She wouldn't do this," Susan said. "I know she wouldn't just leave like this."

"Maybe she'll come back," I said, hopeful. It seemed logical that if Susan said Lorna wouldn't just do this, she wouldn't.

"I didn't say that, either," Susan said, the tears flowing again.

—⟩

With Lorna gone, the dishes piled up. The clothes collected in the hampers. The dust floated in the sunrays and the spiderwebs aggregated in the corners. Grandmother's house, which had once seemed so sunny and sprawling, revealed itself for what it was—an old, musty echo chamber of the settling noises that predicted an end that did not seem so far away.

Grandmother began hand lettering signs that requested the aid of a housekeeper. I couldn't imagine where she'd put them. I couldn't imagine Grandmother hanging up signs with her phone number on them in the middle of town, in the common spaces. But her past channels for finding help had dried up. It was a summer when the people who would have once worked for her were working for themselves, for liberation. I could not then see that Grandmother's view was so far from that liberation as to be a form of shackles. She was my grandmother, with her dusty powdered face and her white hair with a bluish tint that she had styled once a week at the salon, with her hard candies and sweet tea and floppy gardening hat that she wore whenever she was outside; I could not then see her for who she was.

One day, after lettering the signs, Grandmother packed them into an envelope and told me to get ready. Susan, exempt from life in general in her misery, and Jack, exempt because of his age and growing status as what Grandmother called "the man of the house," were not with us. It was only me and Grandmother who walked the long miles in the hot, dry evening after a day that had been too relentlessly sundrenched to complete our task. It was me who held the envelope with the signs as we walked down the dirt roads and then the paved ones closer to the center of town.

We came into the downtown area after winding through the lazy streets around it, the compact houses that seemed so different from Grandmother's house, alone on its own acres as it stood. The downtown, crowded closer than even the close, unseemly houses, had a market and a leather-belt and wallet shop and a shoemaker and a community bank, all pressed up against each other with no room or, by the metrics of Grandmother's sprawling, lonely acres, dignity. I could see Grandmother's own remove from the intimate space in the stiffness of her spine and in her Sunday church clothes (though they were beginning to show signs of heat and sweat from the walk).

Downtown was a mess of cars and people, leaning loosely against buildings and greeting each other on the street. There was a bustle between shops, now that the heat had abated, a counter full of people in the ice cream shop. There were signs in windows that advertised all kinds of things—houses to buy, rooms to rent, jobs that needed to be filled. One said, "Room for let, white tenants in white community." I recall puzzling over it, thinking that communities must be things built like the brick storefronts around me, a piece at a time, with your pieces chosen carefully. It didn't seem any odder to me in the moment that some were all white, just as some storefronts had all red bricks.

There was a board in the center of town where other signs hung. Grandmother marched me past the ice cream shop and toward it, where she took the envelope from my hands. It was only then that she realized she hadn't brought push-pins with her. She scanned the board, tsking and murmuring about the lack of them—each sheet seemed hung by one pin. She searched for an old ad to remove, but finding only current listings, she finally decided that a visit to the hardware store in the corner of one of the crossed roads that marked the center of the downtown was necessary.

We were turning away from the board when we saw that

a woman had been standing near us. She had been watching us, hands on her hips. I grabbed Grandmother's hand instinctively—the woman had Lorna's face, and for a moment I saw hatred in her eyes.

"Yes?" Grandmother said. "Can I help you?"

The woman was holding her own sign, and in the silence that followed, I looked at it. It must have cost her money to make, unlike Grandmother's now embarrassingly hand-lettered one. It was shiny and large, with a picture in the middle and machine-printed words underneath. MISSING, it read in big letters. REWARD FOR INFORMATION.

I realized this was Lorna's mother, not a ghost.

I expected her to slap Grandmother. It was the look in her eyes. So full of rage and righteousness, I found myself thinking that Grandmother *deserved* to be slapped by this woman. The horridness of what I had walked to town for hit me full force then—instead of looking for the woman who had been employed by us, who had disappeared suddenly and without reason—we were looking to fill her spot with a body, to replace her with another mechanism for keeping the house in order.

And here was her mother. Her *mother.* Our housekeeper had a mother, maybe brothers and sisters, a whole life, even beyond the life that I had caught in glimpses, the secret life of romance and forbidden love between her and my sister. Standing there, I began to cry. A child on a dusty hot night, after a dusty long walk, understanding so much more than I could understand, and so much less than was required of some.

The woman looked away from Grandmother and toward me, with something like pity. She walked to the board and hung her sign, walked away.

Even Grandmother seemed to know there was no hanging her hand-lettered sign now. She knew it. But she did it anyway. She walked to the hardware store with her spine stock-straight, bought pushpins, and placed her sign right next to the one Lorna's mother had hung. She jabbed the pin in harder, deeper than it had to go, so that not just the pin but the metal base embedded in the board.

The Sheriff came back a few nights later, and we sat on the porch. The visit did not hold the air of business. He wore his uniform, but was clearly not on duty.

"I think it's time to get them back to Boston, ma'am," he said, sipping Grandmother's tea. "Things here are about to be worse than a divorce. Best they not be here for it."

"I do believe they'll go back when Lanie is ready, and not before," Grandmother said finally.

"The eldest, and the boy," he said. "People are beginning to discuss them."

"People do talk," Grandmother said.

They sat in silence. We sat in silence. The hinkypunk exploded into the night, above the marsh.

"Natural," Grandmother said. "Just a natural thing."

Arrangements were made nonetheless. We were going back north. Grandmother, after much deliberation, had hired an Irish woman from down the road to keep her house. "White trash," she'd whispered, after the woman had called and she had spoken to her. The woman came to work for us a few days later. She packed our bags. She cleaned the house. She missed a cobweb, which Grandmother swatted down crankily, muttering about "Irish curtains."

The night before we were to get on the train, which Susan still seemed unlikely to get out of bed to do, I waited until everyone was asleep. I went down to the marsh. I waited in the dark, near the odor of the brackish water, near the moss and murk, at the edge, for the hinkypunk. It would not appear on command. I didn't know if it would ever appear again. I waited and waited. I thought of my languid sister. I thought of my brother, growing harshly and violently into manhood. I thought of my grandmother. I thought of the missing woman Lorna.

But the hinkypunk never appeared.

We went back to the North, where things were different. Slowly, the summer faded, for me and for Susan. Jack grew longer, leaner, harsher, fighting boys and bringing home beautiful women, one of whom he married when he was twenty-four. Our grandmother came to the wedding, the first time she had been north that I could recall. She was old and frail now, eleven years having aged her twice that amount.

We sat at a family table in an opulent hall. Susan was there, still unmarried, having gone off to college the way she had intended. She lived a life that no one in the family could penetrate, that we could not fathom from our positions. She held us out. I did not wonder why.

"Mother," our mother said after dinner, while we all sat together, "don't you think it's time to give up that old house on the marsh? Move somewhere simpler? That you can manage alone?"

Grandmother deflected again and again, but when our mother persisted, Grandmother's hand slammed down on the table.

"Over my dead body will that house be sold," she said.

The conversation was over.

It did not resume until the groom, my brother Jack, now a fully grown man, so lean and hard and foreign, came to the table.

"My boy," Grandmother said. She put her hand to the side of his face.

They looked into each other's eyes for just a moment. Long enough for me to see the fire there, the unspoken between them, jump and disappear like a hinkypunk.

The Wind, the Wind

for Leonard Cohen

Listen:

There at the end, we took up a collection of all we had left. Gone were the makeshift explosives that had derailed the train, gone were the bullets that had cut down the soldiers who tried to escape, gone was our hope we would make it the six-month lifespan our dearest had. What we had left amounted to some lint, a hard biscuit that we fought for crumbs of, a penny someone had pulled off a dead eye, and our monsters.

We had carried them with us all this way, out to the frontier line where we won the battle but knew our time was short, where the survivors spilled over, in numbers so much greater than ours, and we fell back and hid like ghosts over the graves. First we carried them in our nightmares, then we carried them in our fear, and then we carried them in our anger. Finally, we carried them as our only link to who we were.

They trailed behind us, too far to be seen. We heard the click of their hooves or teeth, looked back for them, saw nothing. But they trailed us always, ragged balloons on too-long strings, clutched in dirty hands.

There at the end, they weren't all that followed us. The soldiers had pursued us since the blast, as had the guns, as had hoary and hungry Death. The soldiers' distance from us on the map shrank, as our stomachs shrank, as whatever force makes life did as well. We felt that force evaporating all around us, rising with the morning mist in the fields, drawing up and away from the skeletons that jutted against our taut flesh.

We lit a fire in an old barn we found destroyed and abandoned on a field. We found and killed a chicken, broke its neck, and pulled its feathers from its dimpled skin. We thanked it for its life, which we would consume and take as our own; Death's nearness had made us spiritual. We felt monstrous as we brought it to its painful, clumsy end. We sealed that end with our myriad prayers. The meat would be barely enough for any strength or energy for any of us, and it seemed so cruel to bring death for so little. But that dwindling force inside us screamed and railed against dissipating, against the urge to lie on the cold ground and never stand back up, to freeze into the landscape.

After we cooked and divided the chicken, after we ate it and the fat of its body still clung to our hands and the whiskers on our cheeks and chins, we warmed ourselves by the fire. Out in the open, we'd had no flames, had not wanted to give ourselves up by their dancing. Here, inside the barn, the fire was close, warm, a sun instead of a surrender. We hunched around it, our old coats smelling of sweat, our thin hands spread at the fingers like starfish above the flames.

We slept that night, really slept, tossing under the weight

of blankets and dreams, burrowing into the hay that still littered the corners and smelled of musky animal hide.

We had been unvigilant in our sleep. When we woke, Death had taken the Romani. His skin was still warm from the fire we had never put out, but stiff and waxen.

He had put his name in our mouths, though none of us were ever to know the others' real names. We had called him worse, the Gypsy, the Gyp, and he'd corrected us each time until he died the Romani to us. We wanted to mourn him, but knew he'd have a better death than us all, better than even the bird we'd eaten for dinner who had thrashed and cried. He had exhaled and escaped on a breath into the mire of dreams, never coming out. All we felt was jealousy.

———

We were across the field the barn stood on when the Romani's monster came walking toward us. It wore his body like a poorly tailored suit. Its teeth were sharp and its skin still the stiff wax of death. We hadn't buried him in his custom for protection; we hadn't removed his head, bound his hands; we hadn't buried him at all. And the monster he had carried had found him, was now carrying him.

His eyes were dead and milky, swimming under the caul of death's second sight. We slowed our pace until he walked with us, his cold bones cracking like gunfire.

———

We kept to the trees after the Romani's monster joined us. Our ammunition long spent, we carried our guns uselessly.

The Romani's monster carried nothing in its hands. Its nails were long yellow daggers, having grown in death and the short walk to us.

Others might have feared, but we carried the penny from a dead eye, the bones of our dinner, our own monsters. We carried the weight of our own skin, growing waxen in the moonrise, breaking and tearing too deep to bleed.

The Romani's monster walked counterclockwise around us as we laid our heads down, dust swirling at its shuffling feet in storm clouds. We coughed deep into our dry lungs and begged it to stop, which it did in time. It lay down flat in the dirt.

The Jew's heart appeared to give out as we shuffled along the dirt road. We didn't know where we were headed any longer except away; our maps had become strange sigils drawn over fantasy mountains. As we tried to walk quietly, the Jew gave out a cry, clutched his chest, and fell. As the warmth spilled from his body, we wrote the names of our gods on paper and slid them under his stone tongue. It had rained the night before, and we streaked his body with mud until he was Adam, the first of his monster's kind.

Mute, unseeing, radioed to commands from who knew where, he rose to follow us.

There were two humans left to walk with the two monsters the dead had carried. We put down our guns.

We knocked on a door and the old woman who answered moved her eyes between us, speaking rapidly in a language none of us spoke. She finally took us, men and monsters, to a shed behind her house. Scolding, it seemed, she brought us dried meats, wine, cheese, bread. We wept and she wept and she and the monsters watched us eat as if we never would again. No politeness or prayer, wolves in our hunger.

We slept among the tools someone had once worked her field with. The monsters walked around the shed.

In the morning, when we rose to say goodbye, she was dead. The monsters couldn't have stopped the single bullet as it went into her head.

The pursuit was almost over.

———

The Madman's monsters came in the night. He let us call him that because his monsters had always called him worse and he had become immune. He was still breathing when they came closer. They huddled beneath the trees, all wet wings, dripping hair, open mouths. Their mouths appeared to chant, though I could not hear them. Only he heard them, as he always had.

I don't know if they chanted his suicide, but his knife flashed silver at his wrists and his blood was an oil slick in the dirt.

The dogs were close, the men were close; I could not bury him, I did not have the strength. So we walked.

And they touched me, one after another: the hand of clay, the long yellow nails with earth beneath them, the claws that rent the skin of my arm.

I wondered who would carry me, as the howling came closer and the torch fire winked with the night stars. My monsters had been amorphous, my histories burned. I wondered if I could claim protection from a fine ghost in a black riding coat, a moon boy sold to a fate he never chose. I thought of the woman who had brought us meat and bread and cheese; I thought of wine dribbling from our lips like blood as we wept and also of her face destroyed by a bullet— the hole of blackness, the well of blood—and I wondered if her spirits could carry me. My vision tunneled as I walked in the dust clouds. There were only the monsters and me, the companions I had found one at a time, with whom I had tried to stop the advance—runaways, escapees, the brutally damned, the unchosen, the cast out. My vision hurled itself to the margins, and I wept and washed away the world, and when I saw again, I saw myself in a shawl, holding a cane. I was an old woman, practicing my old-woman magic on the empty fields, calling the wolves and bears to circle. And the monsters and the bears, the wolves and those mad with frenzy, we turned, we turned, we saw the dogs cower and the torches fall and the wind blow through the graves.

ACKNOWLEDGMENTS

Thanks to my editor and publisher, Dan Simon, who saw the value in these stories, and pushed them to be their best. Thanks to Natalie Kimber, who gave me new hope after a long road. Thank you to the team at Seven Stories Press. Seven Stories is an indie with true radical values, and I am grateful to everyone, from the publisher to the interns there (I was once an intern there myself!). Thanks especially to Allison Paller, Lauren Hooker, and Silvia Stramenga, whose tireless work on *All City* and this book is much of the reason it is in your hands today. Thank you to Dror Cohen and Stewart Cauley, two immensely talented artists it was a pleasure to have work on the design of this book cover. Thanks to the editors who published early versions of these pieces: Gabrielle DiDonato, Sarah Einstein, Tobias Carroll, Phil Sandick, and Lindsay Starck. Thanks to professors and fellow students in my MFA program for their reading and critique: Imad Rahman, Mary Biddinger, David Giffels, Larisse Mondok, Xan Schwartz, Noor Hindi, Elise Demeter, Caroline Knecht, Aimee Bounds, Bridgid Cassin, Beesan Odeh, Sarah Ellen Ford, Sarah Davis, Lauren Olesh, the Barnhouse Collective, and the Sad Kids Superhero Collective. The literary theory book *Gothic* by Fred Botting provided much of the initial spark of inspiration for these stories, and additional inspiration was provided by songs by Leonard Cohen and Jeff Mangum, as well as fiction by Never Angel North, and the tragedy of Rosemary Kennedy's lobotomy. Thanks to John Lurie, my hero and mentor, a true believer in art and its divinity, who has imparted on me lessons about moving forward in the arts with your heart and personal sensibilities above all other things. Thanks to the writer Sawyer Lovett, a brilliant literary friend who generously read early drafts, and for whom I was inspired to write a happy ending. Shout out to the trashy, middle-grade lore, legend, and ghost-story books that were some of my first literary loves, and which I've never grown tired of. Thanks to the baristas at Rising Star and the bartenders at Corky's in Lakewood, Ohio (especially Spencier, Olive, Nikki, and Jorden), who make the best coffee and drinks, compliment my finger tattoos, let me sing Tom Waits at karaoke on busy Saturday nights, and give me a space to work. Thanks to the Lakewood Public Library: I'm sorry I always return books so late, thanks for letting me use your study cubbies anyway. To my new city, Cleveland, which took me in when New York pushed me out, whose emptiness and industrial desolation and bright bursts of life remind me of home in ways that I never imagined possible, and which provides such a canvas for these stories—I imagine, here, vampires and sea witches and gorgons and cryptids moving through the empty spaces. As always, my work wouldn't be possible without my chosen family: Karen and Ed Hutchko; Sarah Baker, Rob Baker, Bella Baker, and Wyatt Baker (and Kaya, Princess Peter, Slasher-Basher, Roxy, Lola, Mr. Sanders, and Ziggy Stardust, their puppies past and present). And a final thank you to my community: you've supported me with love, couches to sleep on, grocery money when I'm broke, meals, cigarettes, and the drive to keep going, no matter how hard things seem. I would be lost without you.

ALEX DIFRANCESCO is the author of *All City* (Seven Stories Press 2019). They have also published fiction in *The Carolina Quarterly*, *The New Ohio Review*, and *Monkeybicycle*. They are a winner of Sundress Academy for the Arts' 2017 OutSpoken contest for LGBTQ+ writing. DiFrancesco's non-fiction has appeared in *The Washington Post*, *Tin House*, *Longreads*, *Brevity*, and was a finalist in Cosmonauts Avenue's inaugural non-fiction prize. Their storytelling has been featured at the Fringe Festival, Life of the Law, the Queens Book Festival, and *The Heart* podcast. DiFrancesco is also a skilled bread baker and pastry cook, a passionate activist and advocate, and has a small, wonderful cat named Sylvia Rivera-Katz.